finish

Realizing That Matt Had Gotten Awfully Quiet, She Glanced Up And Caught Him Staring At The Front Of Her Shirt.

Again. All through dinner he'd been looking at her, undressing her with his eyes.

"They're breasts, Matt. I'm sure you've seen plenty, so mine shouldn't be all that fascinating."

He had the decency to look apologetic. "Sorry, I just can't get used to the way you look now."

"*Different*, right?"

"Good, Em. You look *really* good."

She narrowed her eyes at him. "Let's be clear on something, Conway. Friendship is one thing but I am not, under any circumstances, going to sleep with you again."

Something hot and dangerous sparked in his eyes and her knees instantly went mushy. "That sounds like a challenge, Emily. And you know how much I love a challenge."

Dear Reader,

Welcome to another stellar month of smart, sensual reads. Our bestselling series DYNASTIES: THE DANFORTHS comes to a compelling conclusion with Leanne Banks's *Shocking the Senator* as honest Abe Danforth finally gets his story. Be sure to look for the start of our next family dynasty story when Eileen Wilks launches DYNASTIES: THE ASHTONS next month and brings you all the romance and intrigue you could ever desire…all set in the fabulous Napa Valley.

Award-winning author Jennifer Greene is back this month to conclude THE SCENT OF LAVENDER series with the astounding *Wild in the Moment*. And just as the year brings some things to a close, new excitement blossoms as Alexandra Sellers gives us the next installment of her SONS OF THE DESERT series with *The Ice Maiden's Sheikh*. The always-enjoyable Emilie Rose will wow you with her tale of *Forbidden Passion*—let's just say the book starts with a sexy tryst on a staircase. We'll let you imagine the rest. Brenda Jackson is also back this month with her unforgettable hero Storm Westmoreland, in *Riding the Storm*. (A title that should make you go hmmm.) And rounding things out is up-and-coming author Michelle Celmer's second book, *The Seduction Request*.

I would love to hear what you think about Silhouette Desire, so please feel free to drop me a line c/o Silhouette Books, 233 Broadway, Suite 1001, New York, NY 10279. Let me know what miniseries you are enjoying, your favorite authors and things you would like to see in the future.

With thanks,

Melissa Jeglinski

Melissa Jeglinski
Senior Editor
Silhouette Desire

Please address questions and book requests to:
Silhouette Reader Service
U.S.: 3010 Walden Ave., P.O. Box 1325, Buffalo, NY 14269
Canadian: P.O. Box 609, Fort Erie, Ont. L2A 5X3

The Seduction Request

MICHELLE CELMER

Published by Silhouette Books
America's Publisher of Contemporary Romance

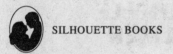 SILHOUETTE BOOKS

ISBN 0-373-76626-2

THE SEDUCTION REQUEST

Copyright © 2004 by Michelle Celmer

Books by Michelle Celmer

Silhouette Desire

Playing by the Baby Rules #1566
The Seduction Request #1626

MICHELLE CELMER

lives in southeastern Michigan with her husband, their three children, two dogs and two cats. When she's not writing or busy being a mom, you can find her in the garden weeding or curled up with a romance novel. And if you twist her arm real hard you can usually persuade her into a day of power shopping.

Michelle loves to hear from readers. Visit her Web site at www.michellecelmer.com, or write her at P.O. Box 300, Clawson, MI 48017.

To R.D.R.
We miss you.

One

"**D**ress it up however you like, Conway, but behind all your money and fame, you'll always be trailer trash to the people of this town."

The line went dead and Matt Conway snapped his cell phone shut, fighting off a sense of unease. He should have expected his homecoming would ruffle a few feathers, that some people from his past would never accept him, yet it still stung. Despite everything he'd accomplished, he felt like a vulnerable kid again.

Shaking off the all-too-familiar sensation, he clipped the phone on his belt and gazed around the partially constructed restaurant interior, dragging a bandana across his sweaty brow. He breathed in the scent of freshly cut pine, waiting to feel the satisfaction, the deep sense of accomplishment he'd more than earned. This was to be restaurant number twenty in the Touchdown Bar and Grill chain, yet this one erected in his hometown of Chapel, Michigan, held special meaning. It was a symbol.

The kid who'd grown up on the wrong side of the tracks now owned sprawling homes in three different countries. He'd traded in the beat-up vehicle of his youth for a medley of vintage cars any collector would salivate over. He had achieved nearly every financial goal he'd set for himself.

So why, he wondered, would a man who had accomplished everything he'd set out to do feel this...*dissatisfaction?* Why would he feel deep down that he was still, as his mystery caller had so succinctly put it, trailer trash. He worked longer hours, pushed himself to the absolute limit, yet that gratification, that feeling that he'd finally arrived, eluded him.

He was sure this restaurant would be the key. If he ever finished it, that is. Each day dawned with a new problem to delay construction further. They were set to open on Labor Day, only two months away, and were already three weeks behind schedule. He had too much riding on this. While there was always the possibility a restaurant could fail, the odds were stacked against him this time.

Chapel, Michigan, population ten thousand, wasn't exactly known for its trendy night spots. Touchdown would either bring in patrons from surrounding areas and boost revenue for the city, or it would flop within the first year.

It was a risk he was willing to take. A risk he *had* to take.

Someone called his name, and he turned toward the voice, grinning when he spotted his best friend,

Tyler Douglas, standing in the doorway. Ty cleared the space between them in two long strides and pulled Matt into a bear's embrace, slapping him hard on the back. "Damn it's good to see you. What's it been, almost six months since I visited California?"

"At least that."

"So how does it feel? Your first return home in what, eleven years?"

"Things have changed a lot." But not so much that he didn't get the same feelings of inadequacy. The impression that when people looked at him, they would forever see his parents. In California, people saw a man who had everything he could possibly want.

Honestly, he couldn't decide who was more disillusioned.

"I should have known you couldn't sit around and watch without getting your hands dirty." Ty spun in a slow circle. "They've come a long way since construction started."

"Thanks for keeping an eye on things for me. And I can't thank you and your parents enough for selling me the property. I know it's been in your family for a long time. Sitting right on Main Street, I couldn't ask for a better location."

"Are you kidding? You're part of the family." Ty leaned against a stud that would eventually support the wall separating the dining area from the game room. "As a matter of fact, that's sort of why I'm here. I have an important favor to ask."

"Anything," he said without hesitation. "Just name it."

"I want you to seduce my sister."

Matt's heart skipped a beat—then it felt as though

it had stopped beating altogether. If there was a last woman in the world he wanted to seduce—or more to the point, *should* seduce—it was Ty's sister Emily. "You're kidding. Right?"

Ty's expression was serious. "I know you guys had some kind of falling out before you left for California, but before you say no, hear me out."

"Falling out" was a mild way of describing what had transpired between himself and Emily. More like, he'd broken her heart and deserted her. But to have led her into thinking there was hope of a relationship would have been dishonest. Despite what he'd felt for her, she deserved more than he was willing to give. And though they'd vowed to remain friends, things had never quite been the same after their one night together.

He'd never been the same.

But it wouldn't hurt at least to hear Ty out before he said hell no. He crossed his arms over his chest and took a seat on an unoccupied sawhorse. "I'm listening."

"There's a problem with Emily's boyfriend."

A sensation that felt too much like jealousy soured his stomach. Of course Emily would have a boyfriend. She was a grown woman. Did he really think she'd been in limbo all these years, unable to love anyone but him?

Well, a guy could hope…

No. He shouldn't hope things like that. He didn't. He wanted Emily to be happy. She deserved to be happy. "What kind of problem?" he asked Ty.

"I know she wants to get married and have a family, but this guy is in no hurry to commit. It's a dead-end relationship. I think deep down she's unhappy but isn't ready to admit it to herself. I'm sure it'll only take a nudge and she'll realize the mistake she's making. That's where you come in.''

''What am I supposed to do?''

''Spend time with her. Show her how much happier she could be without him. My parents and I have tried to talk to her about it, but you know how stubborn she can be. She'll stay with the guy on principle alone if it proves us wrong.''

''Ty, I'm not in the market for a wife and family. If that's what she's looking for, she's not going to find it in me, and I won't lie.''

''I'm not asking you to lie. By all means be honest with her.''

''I'm a little fuzzy on the seducing concept. How far do you expect me to take this?''

''As far as you have to.''

Matt could hardly believe what Ty was suggesting. ''We are talking about the same Emily, right? Your twin sister. The same sister guys were afraid to ask out in high school for fear you would break their legs? *That* Emily?''

''You know, you could try just being her friend.''

And suppose a friendship wasn't enough? It hadn't been back then. And though hurting Emily in the past had been unavoidable, he didn't want to hurt her again. He hated the idea that she was unhappy, but he wasn't necessarily the man to remedy that.

Ty's tone turned dark. ''There is something else. My parents and I have reason to believe this guy might be into something illegal. He and Emily work together. If he's caught, she could be guilty by association.''

Apprehension raised the hair on the back of his neck. "Illegal how?"

"He owns a nursery. They have shipments coming in constantly from all over the world and he's always going out of the country on business."

Genuine fear clenched his gut. "Drugs?"

"That was our first thought."

"So tell her you're suspicious."

"What, and you think she would actually believe me? This is Emily we're talking about. The queen of I'm right and you're wrong. She would laugh in my face."

Matt cursed under his breath, and growled, "Let's just beat the guy within an inch of his life and *make* him break up with her."

"And you know exactly what Emily would do."

He did. She was so damned stubborn she would stay with the guy just to spite them.

"Emily doesn't do anything halfway. If she breaks off the relationship, there's no way she'll keep working with him and the problem will be solved." Ty's tone turned pleading. "If you won't do it for me, do it for my parents."

When Ty put it that way it was difficult to say no. Growing up, the Douglases had been Matt's only real family. He'd shared countless dinners with them, slept over a thousand times, had even gone with them on family vacations. When his own parents couldn't pull themselves out of a drunken stupor long enough to buy something as basic as new tennis shoes, Ty and Emily's parents always seemed to find a pair— brand new no less—lying around the house that just happened to be the right size.

Matt owed them. And God knows he owed Emily.

If Ty was right about her boyfriend, it would be worth the sacrifice. No one was going to mess with Emily and live to tell about it as long as he was around.

"I'll do it," he told Ty. "Just tell me when and where."

Emily Douglas pulled the company truck into a parking spot, cut the engine and peered through the windshield at the partially constructed building. Touchdown Bar and Grill was all anyone in town seemed to talk about lately, and honestly, she didn't see what all the fuss was about. And despite her vow to never set foot within its sport-memorabilia-swamped bowels, here she was.

Swell.

If there had been any way to pass this job off to someone else, she'd have done it. But with Alex out of town, and as manager of the nursery, it was her direct responsibility to give his royal highness, the millionaire, the estimate on landscaping. To add to an already miserable situation, this could be the account to pull Marlette Landscape out of its recent financial distress. She would never forgive herself if she blew this. And Alex, her wayward boss, would never live down the failure of driving the family business into bankruptcy. He meant well, he just had no head for business, and frankly, Emily was growing tired of covering his butt.

In another six months it would be out of her hands. She would have the money to buy the property from her father, then she could get a business loan for the building and her dream of owning her own flower shop would become a reality. But she would never raise the money without a job. She *needed* this account. The commission would push her that much closer to her goal. She would sacrifice just about anything, including her pride, to see it through.

And wouldn't Matt—*People*'s sexiest restaurateur—be surprised to see her darkening his doorway? She'd done a fair job of avoiding him the past eleven years. Not difficult, considering Mr. I Only Date Supermodels Now never came back to Michigan to visit the little people. Apparently the phrase, "I'd still like us to be friends," fell from his lips as readily as the sweet words he'd whispered to her that night on the beach. He hadn't meant those either.

But this was business. She had to put aside what had happened all those years ago and act like a professional.

Yet, as she reached for the door handle, a flare of nerves heaved her stomach into turmoil.

What would he be like after all these years? As a teenager he'd been cocky and arrogant. At least, that's what he'd wanted people to think. He'd never come right out and admitted it, but she knew he was ashamed of his family and probably as insecure as she'd been. That common thread had bound them and kept them close. But he wasn't poor anymore. She was sure the vulnerable kid who hid behind the bravado, the Matt she'd been friends with, was long gone. Oddly enough, the thought made her sad.

The sun burned white-hot overhead and sweat trickled down her cheek. No point sitting here melting. The sooner she got in there, the sooner she could leave.

She stuck out her chin, shoved open the truck door and stepped down. Sweaty male construction types in varying degrees of undress gave the site an interesting atmosphere, but she didn't see anyone resembling Matt. Aware that more than a dozen pairs of eyes were suddenly riveted in her direction, she held her head high, prayed she wouldn't stumble over her own feet, and walked through the open door of the restaurant. It took her eyes a minute to adjust in the dim light, then she scanned the interior and—

No one was there.

Any apprehension she'd been feeling was instantly replaced by a ripple of irritation. Granted, her time wasn't as valuable as his, but he could at least have the courtesy to show up when he made an appointment.

"Emily?" someone said from behind her. "Emily Douglas, is that you?"

She froze in place and her heart started doing a crazy dance in her chest. She knew that voice. Its deep baritone rumbled through her, awakening a long-dead awareness.

You're over him, she reminded herself.

She forced herself to turn and face him, confused for a second by the man standing there. Missing was the thousand-dollar suit she'd expected. He was dressed similarly to the other workers, in faded carpenter jeans and a sweat-soaked muscle shirt that clung to his tanned, muscular chest. The nails she'd expected to be manicured were uneven and workworn and she had the feeling his hands were probably calloused as well. Dirt and sweat streaked down his face, a red bandana covered his hair, and dark sunglasses masked his eyes. But that grin was unmistakable. Riding somewhere in between a smirk and a smile, it was burned permanently into her memory. Matt the millionaire was one of the sweaty construction people.

He slipped the glasses off and staring back at her were eyes the deepest, richest shade of brown. She would never forget those eyes—the way they'd looked at her that night. The tenderness they'd held. And the regret she'd seen there the next morning.

"Emily Douglas." He looked her up and down, as if awed by the sight of her. "I barely recognized you."

And he looked exactly the same. The charming, boyish good looks of his youth had matured right along with the rest of him. In photos and television interviews he always seemed larger than life. An icon. In person, standing here in front of her, he looked like the same old Matt.

A dull ache wrapped itself around her heart and wouldn't let her breathe.

This is business, Emily reminded herself. Just do your job.

"You called for an estimate?" she asked.

An estimate?

Matt stood there, robbed of his voice, completely mesmerized by the woman standing before him. When she'd climbed out of the truck, her legs a mile long, her backside curved under snug khaki shorts, he'd just about forgotten his own name. Oh, man, why hadn't Ty warned him? The rough-and-tumble tomboy was now one-hundred-percent, heart-stopping female.

Unable to do little more than gape, he took it all in, from the pale-blond hair he'd once feathered his fingers through, down the column of her throat to the softly rounded breasts that had fit so perfectly in his palms. His gaze traveled lower, to the toned stomach he'd pressed kisses to, and her legs...*damn.* They were long and trim and looked as smooth as the finest Italian silk. And if memory served, they were. He could still distinctly recall how they'd felt wrapped around him.

When she'd first emerged from the truck, he'd been sure they'd sent the wrong person. It had been Ty's idea to call the nursery where Emily worked, under the guise of needing plants—which Matt really did need. He'd made it clear he would not, under any circumstances, lie to Emily or mislead her in any way.

Emily's expression turned wary. "You did call for an estimate."

"An estimate," he repeated, wondering where his brain had wandered off to. This wasn't going at all as planned. He could barely string a coherent sentence together. He hadn't expected to feel this way. Of course, Emily always did have a way of making him feel things he shouldn't.

"Sorry," he said. "I'm just a little surprised to see you. You look...different."

Her eyebrow quirked slightly. "*Different?* Gosh, Conway. I'm...flattered."

"I didn't mean it like—"

"Look. I realize this is uncomfortable for both of us, but I have a job to do. Let's try to make the best of an inconvenient situation. Okay? I'll get you your estimate and get out of your life."

Damn. This was going to be a little harder than he'd expected. But he had never been one to back down from a challenge. Especially when the stakes were so high. All he needed to do was figure out an angle. Every woman had a weakness. Jewelry, furs, whatever.

Once he determined Emily's, he'd have her eating from his hand.

Two

Matt took a step toward Emily. Close enough to catch a light, flowery scent drifting off her skin. The last time he'd been this close to her, they'd both smelled of the bonfire her father had built on the beach, the fire they sat by long after Ty and Emily's parents had gone to bed.

Back then he'd never imagined Emily wearing perfume. It had always been too girly, too feminine for someone like her. Now it was perfect. *She* was perfect. Just the right height, the ideal combination of lean muscle and female softness. Expressive blue eyes deep enough to drown in.

Or freeze him solid, as they were doing now.

"Well?" Emily tapped her booted foot in the dirt.

"Whatever you want," he said.

"Great." She plucked a pen from her shirt pocket and jotted something down on the form attached to her clipboard. "What were you thinking about for the interior? Ferns? Philodendrons? Real or silk? Is there a particular theme you follow in all the restaurants?"

"I have a binder with all the specs." He gestured to the door and she started toward it, distinctly aware of his presence behind her. *Too* close behind her, she realized as he reached past her to open the door and his sweat-slicked arm brushed hers. No expensive cologne for him today. He smelled like a man who was no stranger to physical labor.

He smelled *good.*

She squinted against the sudden shaft of sunlight slanting across her face as she stepped outside.

"Hey, boss!" One of the workers waved Matt over. "The inspector is here. We got a problem."

"Give me a minute," he called and turned to Emily. "I've got the stuff in my car."

She followed him to a dusty black SUV parked next to the construction trailer. Honestly, she'd expected something convertible and red with an anorexic blonde permanently fixed in the front seat for that special touch.

He opened the passenger's-side door and grabbed a binder off the front seat. "This has photos of the other restaurants and all the information you'll need. The inside plants should all be live. No silk or plastic. Does your company handle maintenance?"

"No, but we can recommend someone." She flipped through the binder, surprised by what she saw. While a few of the older members of the city council had been openly opposed to building yet another unsightly bar in town—and others had protested out of what she was sure was jealousy—Emily had to admit, Touchdown wasn't a bad-looking place. Classy in fact, but casual enough to stop in for a beer and a bite after work. It might even bring in business when her flower shop went up on the vacant lot next door.

"We like to keep the landscaping consistent," he said.

She flipped past a photo that was obviously Southern-based. "I hate to disappoint you, but you'll be hard-pressed to find a palm tree that will grow in Michigan."

The edge of his mouth quirked up slightly. "As consistent as the climate will allow. Now, if you'll excuse me for a minute?" He nodded in the direction of the men waiting for him.

"Go for it."

"Give me a holler if you need anything."

Emily jotted a few notes on her clipboard, watching Matt in her peripheral vision. He might be dressed like the other men and was unshaven and dirty like them, but he had an air about him that garnered respect—*demanded* it even. The intelligence shining behind his eyes, the way he looked at a person, as if he could see inside their head.

He used to look at her that way. Sometimes she swore he could read her thoughts. How many times had she silently willed him to kiss her, to tell her she was anything but a pal? She would wish so hard for it, her head would hurt and her eyes would sting. But he'd never treated her as anything but a good friend.

Someday he would see, she'd told herself at least a thousand times. But Matt didn't date girls like her. He preferred cheerleaders—the pretty girls. Still, she took it for granted that he would always be around, that someday she would get her chance. Then he'd earned a football scholarship that guaranteed he'd be taken away from her forever.

Every time he talked about leaving Michigan, about getting a new start in California and never looking back, a piece of her heart would die. She'd been in love with him since the third grade when his family had moved to Chapel. She could barely remember a time when he wasn't around. He was like family.

To Emily, he had been her whole world.

But as the end of that final summer drew nearer and his leaving loomed closer, something changed. She would catch him watching her, and the look in his eyes, the longing she saw there, would make her shiver with awareness. It was as if she possessed something he desperately wanted, but knew he couldn't have. For the first time in her life she began to feel feminine and pretty. It had occurred to her that maybe he actually had feelings for her and was afraid to make the first move. Though the thought of any female turning down a man like Matt had been completely out of her realm of imagination, she knew he had a vulnerable side he rarely let show. Maybe he was as afraid of rejection as she was.

It was then that she'd decided to tell him how she felt. She knew it wouldn't stop him from leaving— she would never ask him to give up his dream for her—but she'd thought he could come back and visit, and maybe, eventually, she could relocate to California. Yet every time she tried to tell him, she couldn't make herself say the words. Until that last weekend up at the cottage.

Sitting by the fire, she'd finally worked up the nerve to say it. To say "I love you." And before she'd even gotten all the words out he'd kissed her.

She'd given him everything on that beach, surrendered her innocence to him. She woke the following morning feeling lighter than air, until Matt had said they needed to talk. His somber expression—the regret in his eyes—said more than words ever could. Still she'd listened numbly as he explained that while he cared for her deeply—she was his best friend— he was in no position to start a relationship with anyone. He had dreams to fulfill, a new life to start in California. But he still wanted them to be friends. They would *always* be friends. A few days later he left, and, true to his word, he'd never looked back.

Not to her anyway.

Pain, stark and biting, took hold of Emily. She never should have come here. Tears burned behind her eyes and she turned her attention to the estimate forms. She had a job to do.

She walked the perimeter of the building, taking notes and measurements, then went inside and took down the information she needed there. When she stepped back outside, Matt was still deep in conversation with the building inspector. They were bent over what looked like blueprints spread across the hood of a car.

The silly girl in her longed to talk to him again, to search his face for even a glimpse of the Matt she used to love, while the practical Emily convinced her not to bother.

The practical Emily always won.

Matt watched Emily, head lowered as she scribbled something on her clipboard, wondering what was going on in her head, wondering what he was going to do to get back on her good side. Expensive gifts were a favorite of the women he dated, but somehow he couldn't see Emily impressed by glitter. Short of seeing him strung up by his toes and tortured, he wasn't sure what would impress her.

"Mr. Conway?"

Matt tuned to Eric Dixon, the building inspector. "Eric, I've known you since the third grade. Would you please call me Matt?"

Eyes full of contempt, Dixon said, "As I was saying, *Mr. Conway,* the ratio of square feet to lot space is off."

"By twenty lousy feet."

"Regardless, you're either going to have to reduce the amount of square footage or increase the size of the parking lot."

Matt snapped a tight rein on his anger. There was no way he was going to let this weasel get in his way. The restaurant was going up. He would find an angle. He always did. "What I find interesting is that no one mentioned this when the plans were approved. And only now that the structure is half built do you point out the problem."

Eric's smile was smug and full of satisfaction. "It was a regrettable oversight."

One you'll regret more than I will, Matt thought. If they could play hardball, so could he. He took a step toward Eric, amused to see the man take a nervous step back. "I don't suppose this has anything to do with the fact that in high school I beat you out as starting quarterback and got lucky with your girlfriend in the bed of my truck? Didn't you end up marrying her?''

It was only a rumor; he'd supposedly scored with so many of the girls in high school, but it served its purpose. Eric's face turned an interesting shade of purple and the veins in his temple bulged. At twenty-eight, with a beer gut that hung over his belt and nicotine stains on his teeth and fingers, he looked like a heart attack in the making.

"I'm not shutting down construction," Matt said.

"You've got until next week to bring it up to code, then *I'm* shutting you down." Eric slammed his briefcase, and flashed Matt a greasy smile. "Have a nice day."

Though the majority of the city had been supportive of his restaurant, there were a few people who had given him nothing but grief. The same people who'd had so little tolerance for him when he was a kid. No matter how well he did in school, or how he excelled in sports, thanks to his alcoholic parents he'd been labeled a troublemaker by some—guilty by association. Despite his recent fame, living in L.A. afforded him a certain anonymity. In Chapel, a traffic violation won you a spot in the local paper's "Police Beat" column.

He hadn't let them win back then and he wouldn't let them now.

Matt heard an engine start and turned to see Emily's truck pulling out of the lot. She was leaving before he'd had a chance to smooth things over. He felt as if he was being pulled in a dozen different directions at once.

He watched her truck disappear around the corner

and felt more determined than ever to make amends. The only question was, how?

He was pretty sure there would be groveling involved.

"Look at you," Emily scolded. "If you don't pull it together, you'll never get out of this place. There's a sunny window somewhere out there just waiting for you."

The *Abutilon hybridum,* commonly known as a Canary Bird Flowering Maple, sat on the isolation table near the rear of the nursery, looking wilted and sick, its leaves pale and drooping pathetically. Emily plucked an errant brown leaf. "It's not aphids and I don't see a fungus."

She checked the undersides of the leaves for signs of mites. "Your brothers and sisters are healthy. What's the deal?"

"Do they ever answer you?"

At the unexpected voice, Emily let out a squeal of surprise and spun around. She knew who it was even before she saw Matt standing behind her. Her heart gave an appropriate flutter at the sight of him.

Damn him for always looking so good, for bringing back memories that were better off forgotten.

"In a manner of speaking, they do," she said. "It's been scientifically proven that plants respond positively to verbal stimuli."

He nodded thoughtfully and gestured toward the sickly plant. "Maybe this one is hard of hearing."

She had to stifle a smile. He always did have a good sense of humor, and the ability to make her laugh. He'd been the brightest point in her life. Her life had grown dim since then, but she was used to it. She liked it that way. It was tough for people to hurt you, to disappoint you, if you kept them at arms' length.

"What do you want, Conway?" she asked. "I thought we agreed to stay out of each other's way."

"You have my binder with the restaurant specs and I need it for tomorrow. The decorator has my only other copy."

He'd only wanted his folder. Why would she even think he would want to see her for any other reason than business? Why would he be interested in someone like her when he could have a thousand other women? Beautiful, *feminine* women.

And why did she feel disappointment instead of relief?

"I get it for you and you'll leave?" she asked.

"Scout's honor."

"Stay here, I'll be right back." She brushed past him, far too aware of the energy vibrating from his body, and headed toward the front of the building. The man was a walking powerhouse, and even worse, he knew it. Stepping into her miniscule office, she grabbed the binder off her desk, but as she spun around to leave she slammed hard into Matt's chest. The heat radiating from his skin scorched her and she jerked away, bumping the backs of her thighs against her cluttered desk. "What are you doing in here?"

He reached behind him and closed the door. "Giving us some privacy."

"You said you would leave. You did the Scout's honor thing."

He gave her a wide, toothy grin, looking just like the old Matt. "I was never a Scout."

That was exactly the kind of stunt the old Matt would have pulled. He looked like the old Matt, and he was acting like the old Matt—

No. No way she would let herself even consider that. She didn't want to like him. If she started to like him a little, that might grow into liking him a lot. Then he would leave and she would never hear from him again. No thanks. "What do you want from me, Conway?"

"I just want to talk to you. I've…missed you."

"You *missed* me? That would explain why you stopped calling. Never once visited. Yeah, you sure seemed broken up about it."

"Your parents came out to visit me. You could have come with them."

She'd wanted to. It had torn her to pieces to watch her parents leave, knowing they would see Matt. Knowing how badly she'd wanted to see him, too. And knowing it just wasn't an option. Not if her heart was ever going to heal. "I don't remember getting an invitation."

"You were always welcome."

"Oh, was it one of those mind-reading things us women are supposed to be able to do? I probably should have told you, I was absent the day they taught that in home economics."

Matt gave her a scrutinizing look. "I don't remember you being this cynical."

"I'm being realistic." The phone on her desk rang and she turned to snatch it up. Her mood plummeted even lower when she answered the phone and recognized the voice on the other end.

"Emily, dear," Alex's mother said sharply. "I need to speak with my son."

"I'm sorry, Mrs. Marlette, but Alex stepped out for the afternoon." And tomorrow afternoon, and the one after that.

"This is the third time I've called this week. Haven't you been giving him my messages?"

Emily hated this. She hated lying to save Alex's rear end time and time again. "He's been so busy, he probably just forgot to get back to you."

Busy slathering on the suntan oil and sipping exotic fruit drinks, she wanted to add. He hadn't answered his cell phone or responded to the dozens of pages she'd sent the past three days. She was no stranger to the pressures of a demanding, critical family and understood his need to escape. But without his participation, she wouldn't be able to hold his life together for him much longer.

"Could you please let my son know that the accountant will be out next Wednesday at nine sharp for the quarterly audit and I expect him to be there." The woman's tone was so bitterly cold, Emily was sure she could feel icicles forming on her ear.

"I'll pass the message along, Mrs.—"

There was a click, then the line went dead.

"Nice to talk to you, too," she mumbled as she dropped the phone back in the cradle. If she didn't know the woman better, she might have taken the harsh treatment personally. But Alex's mother regarded everyone, including her own family, with equal contempt.

Emily turned to find Matt leaning against the door, hands tucked loosely in his jeans pockets, watching her.

She gave him her best exasperated look. "Are you still here?"

His grin widened until the hint of a dimple dented his left cheek, raising the boyish-charm-level tenfold. "I haven't asked you out to dinner yet."

"Dinner? You've got to be kidding me."

"It's the least I can do."

She handed Matt the binder. "Goodbye, Conway."

He took it, and something warm in his expression, a glint in his eyes, had shivers crawling up her spine.

He opened the door. "When can I expect an estimate?"

"Give me a week." Maybe by then she would have shaken off this nagging attraction.

"I have one more question," he said.

"I won't go out to lunch with you either."

He grinned and her insides flipped. "How certain can I be that Marlette will complete the job if I accept your bid?"

His question threw her for a moment, then she recognized, like any good businessman, he'd done some digging. Not that he'd have to dig very deep. Marlette's financial difficulties were common knowledge among competing nurseries, several of whom had lowballed them out of many a contract this season. She hadn't yet figured out how, but as low as Marlette kept their bids, there was always someone lower. Though she hoped she was wrong, she was beginning to suspect they had a rogue employee on the loose.

One more thing she didn't have time to worry about.

"This could be the account to save our butts," she said. "If we win the bid, we'll come through for you. You have my word."

"That's good enough for me." Emily's honesty impressed Matt. And what he hadn't mentioned was that Marlette was the only company bidding. He didn't often let sentimentality edge its way into his business dealings, especially with his investors so shaky about the venture, but in this case he was making an exception. Emily was obviously working hard to pull the company into the black. He admired her determination.

Not to mention that this was about the only way she'd let him within a hundred yards of her.

"I look forward to doing business with you." He held out a hand for her to shake. She hesitated a second, then gripped his hand firmly.

Nothing fluffy about that handshake. She was all business, and it was over so quickly he barely had time to relish her soft skin against his fingers.

The phone rang again. She turned to pick it up, and after a pause snapped, "Where in the hell have you been, Alex? I've been trying to get a hold of you for days. Mildred has been all over my back."

The mysterious boyfriend, no doubt.

She listened for a minute, and Matt could swear he heard music over the line. Something Caribbean.

"Hold on, Alex." She cupped a hand over the mouthpiece and turned to Matt. "I need to take this."

"Can I give you a bit of advice?" he asked.

She looked to the door, gave an exasperated sigh, then nodded.

"You'll get nowhere in business cleaning up someone else's mess." With an image of her perplexed expression etched into his mind, he walked out, grinning to himself. Tugging his keys from his pocket, he headed out to the parking lot.

He was wearing her down. As hard as she was working to seem irritated, he could sense her relaxing, letting her guard down. He could also sense her conflict. She wanted to like him, but she was afraid to trust him. It wouldn't be much longer before he had her hooked, and in the meantime, he was enjoying the hell out of himself. For the first time in months he was focused on something other than getting the restaurant built and it was a welcome relief. He would even consider leaving the construction company to its own devices for a day if he could spend the time with Emily.

He thought of the lake up at the cottage where they'd spent so many summer afternoons and wondered if she still liked to fish. Or they could drive to Metro Park, rent bikes and ride the trails. Hell, they could sit on the hood of his car and talk all day for all he cared. As long as he was with her. And maybe, if things went well he could invite her back to his hotel room....

The direction of his thoughts startled him. Taking Emily back to his hotel for...well, whatever they might end up doing, was out of the question. For now. Pushing too hard, too fast, would only drive her away. He had to remind himself, he was doing this for Ty and his parents. If this Alex person was really into something shady, it was imperative Matt not screw this up.

He'd already decided to take Ty's advice and concentrate on being her friend.

Three

The air drifting in the front window, thick and sticky and tinged with the scent of summer rain, zapped the last of Emily's energy. She stretched out on her love seat, waiting for the pizza guy, relieved the day was almost over. As badly as it had begun, when she was convinced things couldn't get much worse, they had.

Alex, it would seem, was having so much fun he'd decided to extend his vacation another few days. She'd tried to explain how difficult it had been holding it together at work lately and he came back with his typical, "Don't worry about it, Em. It'll all work itself out."

He didn't have to face twenty-five employees, not to mention the fifteen or so college kids they hired every spring and summer, knowing it might only be a matter of weeks before they were out of a job. Though he was her good friend and she loved him to death, acting as a human shield between him and his mother was getting old.

The doorbell rang and she rose from her seat, grabbing the ten-dollar bill for the pizza from the coffee table on her way to the door. Money in hand, she pulled the door open, but it wasn't the pizza guy standing outside her apartment. It was Matt.

And she'd be damned if her traitorous heart didn't lift a little at the sight of him. That cocky grin he always wore told her he was up to no good.

She leaned on the doorjamb, trying her best to look annoyed while her lips itched to return the smile. His hair was damp, his chin freshly shaved, and the clean scent of soap and shampoo begged ''notice me!'' Drops of rain spotted his muscle shirt, drawing her attention to the impressive width of his shoulders and the definition in his biceps and arms.

Something hot and feminine stirred deep inside her.

She conjured up her best annoyed voice. ''Are you stalking me?''

From behind his back he produced a large pizza. ''If you won't come to dinner with me, I bring dinner to you.''

''I'm not hungry,'' she lied, and as if on cue, her stomach gave a hollow moan.

''Your stomach disagrees.'' Matt lifted the lid and peeked inside. ''Pepperoni, sausage, bacon—you sure you don't want a slice?''

''How did you know...wait a minute, that's *my* pizza! You rat! You stole my dinner.''

The grin widened, his dimple winking adorably. ''I paid for it, so it is technically mine now. But I'd be willing to share it with you.''

"Is there *anything* you won't do to get what you want?"

"That depends on what I want." The simmering look in his eyes, his smoldering tone, warmed her all the way through to her bones. He didn't even seem to be doing it on purpose. It was as if oozing sex appeal came naturally. Effortlessly.

She crossed her arms over her chest. "How did you even know where I live?"

"CIA."

"That's very funny."

"It's classified. If I tell you, I'll have to kill you."

She glared at him, tapping her foot.

"All right, I asked your brother." He lifted the box lid. "Hmm, smells delicious."

Her mouth watered as the scent wafted her way. She'd skipped lunch so she was beyond starving and there was next to nothing edible in the refrigerator.

"Another minute and you're going to be drooling, Em."

This was so unfair. He knew how much she loved pizza.

"Fine, you can stay." She stepped back and held the door open. Only then did she realize she was wearing her baggy pajama bottoms and the University of Michigan T-shirt with the paint splatters on the front. Like he would even notice.

Or care.

Matt stepped inside, gazing around her one-room flat.

"It's small, but I like it that way," she automatically explained. She had no idea why she felt the need to justify her living conditions to him. Although it might have had something to do with her mother's constant, "Why don't you get a real apartment, Emily," or "If you can't afford a decent place to live, why don't you move back home with us?" As if that would ever happen. Emily would be hauled away in a straitjacket inside of a week.

"I have closets bigger than this," Matt said, then cringed and added, "I didn't mean that like it sounded. I'm just thinking how ridiculous it is that I have so much stuff I need closets the size of an apartment."

He looked so disturbed by the idea, she had to wonder if maybe he wasn't quite as egotistical as she'd thought. Or maybe he was only pretending to be like the old Matt. The question was, why? What could he possibly want from her? Was it possible that he really did want to be her friend?

"When I signed my first pro deal, I had money for the first time in my life," Matt said. "I swear all I did that first year was buy stuff. I guess I just never throw anything away."

"I feel your pain. It must have been real rough having all that money to spend."

"You'd be surprised." His eyes darkened with some emotion she couldn't identify, and she had the sudden impression she'd dredged up something he didn't want to confront. She couldn't decide if that was a good or a bad thing.

Probably bad.

She grabbed paper plates and napkins from the kitchenette and opened the fridge. "I suppose you'll want something to drink."

"Whatever you've got," he said, looking around as if he wasn't sure where to put the food.

"I usually eat at the coffee table, so I can see the

game.'' And because it happened to be the only table she owned.

"Still a sports fan, huh?" He set the pizza down and sat on the love seat.

She grabbed two beers. "To my parents'-dismay. My mother is always trying to drag me to Junior League meetings and Tupperware parties, when I'd rather stay home and watch the game with Ty and my dad.''

She set the beers, napkins and plates on the table and sat next to him. Matt served them each a slice of pizza. Somehow the love seat felt a lot smaller with him sitting on it. They were so close, she could feel the heat of his thigh where it almost touched her own.

Though it was eons ago, she still remembered what it felt like to be close to him. To feel those hard planes of muscle in his chest and stomach, his weight pressing her into the cool sand. Being with Matt had been everything she'd ever imagined—more than she'd ever hoped for. It had scared her as much as it thrilled her. And the tenderness he'd shown her had been completely unexpected. Foolishly she'd thought that meant he loved her.

After all they'd been through together, when all was said and done, she'd been nothing but a conquest to him. All those years of friendship had meant nothing. And now, with all that money he couldn't spend fast enough, she was sure he'd also raised his standards. She was the same unfeminine, in-your-face-girl she'd been back in high school. She hadn't been good enough for him before, and she certainly wouldn't be now, even if she wanted to be. Which she absolutely did not.

"Ty mentioned that you have a boyfriend. My being here won't bother him?" Matt asked.

Boyfriend. Now there's a term she used rather loosely. It wasn't as if she'd actually told her parents she and Alex were anything but good friends. They'd assumed, and she'd never set them straight.

"No, he wouldn't mind. He's not the jealous type." Not when it came to women, anyway. Not only was Alex not her significant other, he was very gay. Flaming at times.

Matt looked down, suddenly enthralled by his pizza. "I'd like to meet him. You should bring him around the restaurant some time."

Emily almost laughed. "You still can't lie worth a damn, Conway."

His head shot up, a combination of guilt and surprise on his face.

"My brother can't stand Alex. And he probably told you that. So I seriously doubt you're all that jazzed about meeting him."

"You work with him?"

"His mother owns the nursery."

Matt gazed around the apartment. Considering her living conditions, this guy obviously wasn't paying her enough. What furniture she did have looked hand-me-down, and with the exception of the twenty or so plants hanging throughout the apartment, it was sparsely decorated. No art hanging on the walls. No photos.

Ty hadn't been exaggerating. This boyfriend of Emily's did sound like a jerk. Abandoning Emily and leaving her to run his mother's company while he was out partying was pretty low. And with a girlfriend as attractive as Emily, how could the guy not be jealous when she invited other men into her apartment? If Emily were Matt's girlfriend, she wouldn't be hanging out with other men. And she wouldn't be living in a matchbox. She would have the best of everything—anything her heart desired.

If she were his *girlfriend?*

Where the hell had that come from? As unfit as this Alex guy was for Emily, Matt was no more properly suited. God only knows where he'd squeeze her into his schedule.

His cell phone rang and Matt checked the display, cursing under his breath. His lawyer. He was awaiting information on the code-violation issue. This could be either really good or really bad news.

"I have to take this."

He answered the phone, and, as he'd expected, it wasn't what he wanted to hear. The violation was legitimate, and their only recourse at this time would be to meet the inspector's demands, or file a lawsuit against the city. Suing Chapel would guaranty the restaurant's failure.

Emily made an impatient noise beside him and Matt had the feeling she wasn't thrilled with the interruption. Now was not the time to be getting on her bad side. Though it was against every principle of business he'd learned, he told his lawyer he'd call him back later, shut the phone off and hooked it back on his belt.

"Sorry about that," he said.

"So, Conway." Emily twisted the top off her beer. "You've got me here. What do you want?"

"What do you mean?"

She took a bite of her pizza and washed it down with a swallow of beer. "After eleven years and no word from you, there has to a reason why you've suddenly popped back into my life.''

He'd thought he'd be able to flub his way through this and skirt around the truth. She never had been one to sit back and let life happen around her. He should have known she would come right out and bluntly ask him what he was up to. He should have expected it.

''I'm reconnecting,'' he said, which wasn't completely untrue. ''The relationships I've been finding myself in lately have been…unsatisfying.''

''What's wrong, the California girls aren't putting out? Or have you slept with them all already?''

''No, there are a few I've yet to violate.'' Out of the corner of his eye, he saw the edge of her mouth lift. ''By unsatisfying, I mean shallow.''

''So what, you expected to come back and just pick up where you left off?''

''That was sort of the plan. I'd like us to be friends, Emily.''

She made a huffing sound. ''I'm not crazy about your definition of friendship, Conway.''

''Look, I know I should have kept in touch. You probably won't believe this, but I never wanted to hurt you.''

''But you did.''

The accusation felt like a knife in his gut. He pushed his plate away, his appetite a memory. ''People make mistakes. You could cut me a little slack.'' The second the words were out, when her eyes turned stone-cold, he knew it was a mistake.

She got up and walked to the door, pulled it open and motioned outside. ''Goodbye.''

''You're kicking me out?''

"I said you could stay for dinner. And I don't know about you, but I've lost my appetite."

He rose from the love seat, balling his napkin and tossing it onto the table. "You were never one to play games, Emily."

"I'm not the one playing games, Conway."

He had a lot of nerve, coming here, manipulating her, then accusing *her* of playing games. He wanted her to cut *him* some slack. She wasn't the one who'd stopped writing, stopped calling. She wasn't the one who'd stayed away for eleven years.

She opened the door wider.

"Is this your way of saying you don't want to be friends?"

"I *was* your friend. That's one mistake I won't be making again."

This time her heart might not survive.

Emily rested her head against the lush ivy twining the cedar arbor, inhaling the sweet scents of her mother's flower garden. Amber clouds streaked the sky as the sun dipped below the horizon and a warm breeze caressed her face. Ordinarily, surrounding herself with nature worked like a salve on her frayed nerves, but it was family dinner night at her parents' house.

Her least favorite, and most nerve-racking Friday of the month.

Nothing short of hospitalization or death held up as a legitimate excuse to miss it. Her parents liked to stay actively involved in her life, which equated to two hours of them telling her exactly what she was doing wrong and how to fix it, while Emily smiled, nodded and tried not to scream. Not that she didn't love her family dearly, but she'd given up trying to please them a long time ago.

And, as if spending the evening with her parents wasn't bad enough, they'd excitedly informed her that Matt was joining them tonight. Given their level of enthusiasm and the extravagant meal her mother was preparing, one might have thought the President was coming to dinner.

She hadn't talked to Matt since he'd left her apartment last night. And while she would never admit it aloud—she didn't even like admitting it to herself— she had hoped he would come back.

Shortly after he'd left she'd gone to bed, listening to the rain tap against the front windows and feeling inexplicably lonely. Every time she heard a vehicle approaching, or the slam of a car door, she'd held her breath, waiting to hear footsteps up her walk. But he hadn't come. And though she hated herself for it, she still missed him somewhere deep down.

Back when they were kids, during summer vacations when Matt was practically living at their house, he and Emily would sometimes stay up all night talking. After everyone had gone to bed, they would go out on the back patio, curl up in chaise lounges and talk until the sky turned pink with the first hint of dawn. There wasn't a thing about each other they hadn't known.

She'd never blamed him for what had happened between them that night on the beach. She'd let it happen, with no second thoughts and no regrets. She only regretted that it had ended their friendship. It was too late to get that back. They had both changed too much.

Sure, he looked the same, and sounded the same

and sometimes he even acted like the old Matt. On the inside, where it counted, he was a different person.

When she'd gotten over the initial shock of his leaving, her heart had begun to heal. And after a while she'd even stopped missing him. Now that he was back, that old longing had returned with him. But she was longing for the friendship of a man who no longer existed.

Behind her on the brick path she heard approaching footsteps. Heavy steps that would indicate the person in question was probably male, and most likely large. Six foot three, two hundred and twenty pounds—most of it muscle—if memory served. She closed her eyes and prayed silently, please let it be someone else.

"Dinner is almost ready." Matt's deep voice wrapped around her, raising the hair on her arms and sending a shiver down her spine despite the heat. "Your mom sent me out to get you."

Thanks, Mom. Without even trying she somehow always managed to make Emily's life a little bit more miserable. "Tell her I'll be right there."

There was a brief silence then, "Emily, come on. You could at least look at me."

Apprehension surging up her throat, she slowly turned. Matt stood, hands tucked casually into the pockets of his pants. At the sight of him, her body sighed with satisfaction. Talk about eye candy. The man was far too attractive for his own good. His hair was damp again and the same near-black shade as his eyes. A hint of his aftershave drifted in her direction, drawing her attention to his chiseled jaw and mouth. And oh, the things that mouth had done to her. Intimate things that still made her blush.

All his features combined, Matt looked rugged and dangerous—which was at complete odds with the conservative polo shirt and chinos he wore. Was it possible for a man to look reckless and sexy wearing Ralph Lauren?

His eyes soft and apologetic, he said, "I screwed up last night."

It was the last thing she expected to hear, and it sounded far too much like something the old Matt would say. Don't, she wanted to plead. Don't you dare be nice to me. She wanted to hate him for leaving her, for not loving her.

But how could she hate him for being honest?

She hugged herself, feeling naked and vulnerable in a simple tank top and shorts. Which was beyond ridiculous, because she wore similar clothes all the time and she'd never felt underdressed before. Maybe it was the way Matt looked at her, as if he were studying every inch, memorizing her.

His cell phone rang and he reached down—she thought to answer it. Instead he turned it off.

"Emily," he said, taking another step toward her. She wanted to turn and run to the house, but she couldn't make her legs move. "I'm sorry I hurt you. I'd do anything to take it back if I could."

She looked for a trace of deceit in his eyes, a sign that he was only manipulating her. All she saw was sincerity, and it put the tiniest crack in the ice covering her heart.

"Can you give me another chance? Can we be friends?"

"For how long, Conway? How do I know you're

not going to go back to California and never call me again? What reason do I have to trust you?"

"None," he admitted. "You have no reason to trust me. I'll have to earn it."

She knew she was losing it when the idea of Matt working to gain her trust gave her a giddy, adolescent thrill. The thrill she used to get every time he smiled at her, or bent his head close to help her bait her fishing line. How many times had she intentionally popped her bike chain off the track for the sheer pleasure of watching him fix it, knowing he was doing something nice for her. And he would do it without question every time. What would he have said had he known she could bait a line with more skill than he could, or tear apart a bike and rebuild it blindfolded.

At times her adoration had been so intense she'd ached with it. But Matt had always been, and always would be completely unattainable. Even now, after everything that had happened, the thought made her inexplicably sad.

"So, what do you say? Tentative friends?" He reached for her, and though she opened her mouth to object, the words died on her lips the second he took her hand. He cradled it gently in his enormous palm. She watched, mesmerized as his thumb brushed across her knuckles. Heat pooled deep in her stomach and her eyelids felt weighted down.

She risked a glance up to his face and found herself instantly locked into his dark gaze. Something sparked deep inside his eyes—a flame she thought had died a long time ago. How could she deny him anything when he looked at her that way?

"Emily! Matt!" Her mother's voice cut through the silence like a guillotine, obliterating the moment.

Emily yanked her hand free, and when he reached for her again, she backed away. "Don't. I need some time to think about this."

"Emily—"

"Just give me a little time."

Matt watched Emily walk briskly down the path toward the house. Though he knew he'd hurt her, he hadn't realized just how badly until that very moment. She was so afraid to be hurt again she wouldn't even risk a friendship with him.

If he could only make her see that his leaving had been for her own good. That he'd been protecting her by breaking all ties. And yes, he'd been protecting himself, too. But last night he realized just how much he'd missed her friendship. He wanted that deep connection back in his life. He yearned for it. But she needed time.

Ironically, time was the one thing he didn't have.

Four

Matt leaned back in his chair, draining the last of his coffee, doing his best not to flinch as the bitter sludge slid down his throat and sat like a rock in his stomach next to the overcooked chicken. "That was an amazing meal, Mrs. Douglas. Thanks again for having me over."

"Aren't you sweet." Emily's mother beamed with pride and reached across the table to pat Matt's hand. "You know you're always welcome, dear."

Beside him Emily, who had been quiet throughout the meal, made a "pfft" sound. Matt glanced over at her, eyebrow raised, and she looked back, the picture of innocence. More than once during dinner Matt had found himself watching her out of the corner of his eye, intrigued by the subtle changes since he'd last seen her. And some not so subtle. Her hair was the same pale shade of blond, but instead of the

short, boyish cut she used to wear, it now hung halfway down her back in silky waves. Her neck was
long and slim, her face thinner, accentuating the high
arch of her cheeks and full mouth. Despite her
height, which he guessed to be at least five-nine, and
the muscle tone that indicated she was no stranger to
vigorous exercise, she was distinctly feminine.

And then there were her breasts. Not too big, not
too small. Not that he had a right to look, but damn,
they were as pretty as the rest of her. He let his gaze
wander down to the front of her tank top, where he
could barely make out the pattern of a lace cup beneath the white cotton.

At the sudden, intense pull of lust, and a death
glare from Emily, he tore his gaze away.

"Hey, Matt, I'll bet you can't get a home-cooked
meal like this in California," Mr. Douglas boomed
from the opposite end of the long dining table.

And thank God for that, Matt thought wryly. Mrs.
Douglas had a heart of gold, but she still couldn't
cook worth a damn. "No, sir, not even close."

"Oh, Phil." Emily's mother waved a hand at her
husband. "Don't be silly. Matt probably has an entire
staff of cooks in that fancy house of his. Don't you,
Matt?"

"I eat out most of the time," he admitted. "And
when I'm home I like to cook for myself. I only hire
kitchen staff when I'm entertaining."

Ty lifted an inquisitive brow. "Entertaining?"

Matt knew exactly the kind of entertaining Ty was
referring to. But it was rare that he invited a woman
home. Most of his relationships were far too superficial and short-lived. "Dinner parties mostly or hol-
iday meals." He turned to Emily's mother and

grinned. "I've yet to find someone who cooks like you do."

"You flatter me," Mrs. Douglas said, her smile radiant. Her face had a taut, stretched look he didn't remember, and he wondered if she'd had some work done.

Emily cleared her throat and Matt could swear she mumbled something that sounded a lot like "brown-noser." He looked over at her but she was sawing at the rock-hard pecan pie.

"Would anyone like a warm-up on their coffee?" Mr. Douglas asked, holding up the carafe.

"There's more pie in the kitchen," his wife added.

"None for me," Ty said. He leaned back and stretched his arms high over his head. "I'm stuffed. I'm gonna go turn on the game."

Emily stood and began gathering the dishes. "My turn to clear and load the dishwasher."

"Don't you even think about it, young lady," her mother scolded. "We *hand*-wash the good china."

"Wonderful," Emily muttered under her breath, shooting Matt a look of contempt, as if it was somehow his fault. Then he realized it probably was. In all the years he'd known the Douglases, they'd used the fine china only on special occasions. He was guessing tonight's special occasion was probably him.

As Emily reached for her mother's plate, Mrs. Douglas grabbed her hand, studying her nails. "For heaven's sake, Emily, look at your fingernails. They're filthy. What happened to the nailbrush I gave you?"

"I was in a rush."

"It's not bad enough you dig around in the dirt

all day, you couldn't have the decency to wash your hands like a lady?''

''I did wash my hands,'' Emily said, calmly tugging her hand away and stacking her mother's plate atop the others. ''Why should I spend an hour scrubbing my nails when they'll just get dirty again tomorrow?''

Mrs. Douglas turned to her husband. ''Phil?''

''Hope, leave the girl alone.'' As Emily picked up her father's plate, he patted her arm. ''Honey, if it makes your mother happy, would it kill you to take a few extra minutes with the nailbrush?''

''No, Daddy, of course not.''

''That's my girl.''

Matt watched the exchange with mounting irritation. Throughout the meal Emily's mother had nagged at her incessantly. It amazed him that after all these years the woman still nitpicked every little thing she did. ''Emily, chew with your mouth closed.'' ''Emily, sit up straight.'' ''No elbows on the table, Emily.'' Emily, Emily, Emily.

It was enough to drive a person crazy, yet Emily seemed immune.

Matt rose from his chair, seeing this as the perfect opportunity to spend some quality time with her—and yes, earn a few brownie points. ''I'll help with the dishes.''

''Emily doesn't need help,'' Mrs. Douglas said sternly. ''You're our guest. We'd love to hear more about your restaurants.''

His restaurants and his social contacts were pretty much all they had talked about during dinner. He was getting bored with the subject, and having a hard time finding anything interesting to say. His life wasn't nearly as exciting as they seemed to think. He worked so many hours lately, he didn't have much of a social life anymore.

He started clearing away the dishes. "I wouldn't mind catching up with Emily."

Emily disappeared into the kitchen and Mr. Douglas shot his wife a look. "Give the kids some time *alone,* Hope."

As if co-conspirators in some secret plot—a plot to lure Emily from her boyfriend, no doubt—Mrs. Douglas gave her husband a wink and smiled at Matt. Though he'd agreed to do exactly that, he felt a jab of resentment on Emily's behalf. They treated her as if she were a child.

He helped Emily clear away the last of the dishes, and when he was sure the rest of the family was tucked away in the other room and out of hearing range, he asked her softly, "Why do you let her do that?"

She turned on the faucet, filling the sink with hot sudsy water while she scraped the plates off into the garbage. "Do what?"

"Nag you like that. It wasn't even me your mother was riding and I wanted to stuff a napkin in her mouth."

"I barely notice anymore." She held up a dishrag and towel. "Wash or dry?"

He took the towel. "How can it not bother you?"

"I suppose it gets annoying sometimes, but I've learned to tune a lot of it out." She submerged the plates in the soapy water, then dumped a pile of silverware in with it and started washing. "Is that why you're hiding in here with me and not out regaling them with tales of your jet-set lifestyle?"

"My life isn't nearly as glamorous as everyone thinks." He plucked a plate from the drain board, rubbed it dry and set it on the counter. "And I am *not* a brownnoser."

She propped her hands on the edge of the sink and looked up at him, her expression pure sass. "'That was an amazing meal, Mrs. Douglas,'" she mimicked. "What's amazing is that we don't all have ulcers. My mother is and always has been a lousy cook."

"Ah, but I was being polite," Matt said. "It's all in the delivery."

She rolled her eyes up. "Oh, please."

"It was the truth. I've never met anyone who cooks like her." And, he hoped, he never would. "I don't know why they're making all this fuss over me."

She slanted him a sideways glance. "I don't suppose it would have anything to do with you being a celebrity."

He grimaced at the label. "I own a couple of restaurants, so what?"

"Last I heard it was closer to twenty. And let's not forget that you're a millionaire."

He shrugged, taking the serving platter after she'd rinsed it. "I made a few smart investments, I have a good business manager."

"Okay, you're an ex-football star."

"I was not a star. I wasn't even the starting quarterback. My pro career was just beginning when I blew out my knee. Nothing impressive about that."

"*People* magazine?" she said and he grimaced again. "You can't deny that was an attention grabber."

Which is why he'd been so against it when his publicist had called to break the good news. "It was a business decision."

She handed him a dripping wineglass and their fingers touched. She felt it like an electric surge, the soapy water acting like a superconductor. It took all her concentration not to snatch her hand away. Don't let him know, she warned herself. As soon as he figures out you want him, you'll be toast.

"And I'll bet you didn't get a single date from the exposure," she said.

"Would you believe me if I said no?"

Jeez, did he think she was completely naive? She'd seen that magazine; Matt decked out in tight, threadbare blue jeans, his white shirt unbuttoned exposing his wide, muscular chest and deeply tanned skin. His hair was a little messy, as if he'd just taken a romp with his favorite Playboy Bunny. And the "come hither" look on his face, the heat in his dark eyes; it gave her shivers just to imagine it.

She sank her hands deeper into the sink to scrub the silverware, the hot water making her feel edgy and overheated. Or it could have been Matt. Actually, it probably *was* Matt.

The adolescent affection she used to feel for him, the giddy, excited sensation she would get in the pit of her stomach every time she saw him had evolved over the years. This new, hot-all-over, weak-kneed desire felt a lot more like lust. Fortunately, lust was superficial and without substance. It could be ignored—if he weren't standing less than a foot away from her oozing sex appeal and smelling like a million bucks.

"I didn't want to do the photo shoot," Matt said,

and it took Emily a second to remember what they had been talking about. Magazine photo. Right.

She rinsed a handful of silverware and dropped it in the drain board. "So why did you?"

"The truth is, the restaurants weren't catching on the way I'd hoped. I could potentially have lost millions. My publicist thought it might boost business."

"Did it?"

"Within the next three years, I'll be opening five more restaurants."

"You should be really happy then," she said, scrubbing a plate with more vigor than necessary. "Being filthy rich is what you've always wanted."

He was silent for a minute, then he laughed. "You're threatened by my money."

"That's ridiculous," she said, the denial coming automatically.

"No, I could see it in your eyes when you walked into the restaurant the other day. You were on the defensive. You think because I have money, I'm a different person."

Though she wanted to, she couldn't deny it. All these years, she'd just assumed money had changed him. Could she have been wrong? Could it be that this was her Matt, the Matt who had once been as integral a part of her life as the air she breathed? Her mind wrapped itself around the possibility, trying it on for size.

He leaned close and cupped her chin in his hand, turning her to face him. "It's still me, Em. I'm still here."

Right then she had the wildest urge to kiss him. She wanted it so bad she even leaned in the tiniest bit, but came to her senses at the last minute and pulled away. "I guess that remains to be seen," she said instead. He might be the old Matt, but that didn't mean he was incapable of hurting her again. In fact, it made the chances even greater that he would.

He cleared his throat. "So, about the friendship thing…"

"I'm still thinking."

"Come on, Em." He gave her shoulder a nudge. "You know you can't resist me."

"You're right, you haven't changed. You're still an incurable egomaniac."

He gave another one of those grins, the kind that softened her tough, outer shell. "See, I told you I haven't changed."

She suppressed the smile that was itching to creep across her face. Grabbing the scrub brush, she started in on the pan her mother had cooked the chicken in, deciding almost immediately that she would need a sandblaster to loosen the blackened goo clinging to the bottom. She put it aside and grabbed a bowl instead.

Realizing that Matt had gotten awfully quiet, she glanced up and caught him staring at the front of her shirt. Again. All through dinner he'd been looking at her, undressing her with his eyes.

"They're breasts, Matt. I'm sure you've seen plenty, so mine shouldn't be all that fascinating."

He had the decency to look apologetic. "Sorry, I just can't get used to the way you look now."

"*Different,* right?"

"Good, Em. You look *really* good."

She narrowed her eyes at him. "Let's be clear on something, Conway. Friendship is one thing but I am not, under any circumstances, going to sleep with you again.''

Something hot and dangerous sparked in his eyes and her knees instantly went mushy. ''That sounds like a challenge, Emily. And you know how much I love a challenge.''

The bowl she'd been washing slipped from her fingers and splooshed down into the sudsy water. She turned away so he wouldn't see the rush of color in her cheeks. ''I'm sorry to disappoint you, but I'm not the least bit attracted to you anymore.''

''Here, let me help you with that.'' He stepped behind her and slid his arms into the water next to hers. The width of his chest spread heat across her back and every feminine nerve ending in her body screamed to life. His hands folded over hers, fingers linked with her own and her temperature shot up what felt like a thousand degrees.

If there had ever been a question that Matt still desired her the evidence was blatantly clear when he leaned in closer, pressing her against the edge of the counter with the lower half of his body. The firm ridge beneath his jeans took her breath away.

''Remember what it was like, Em? Remember what it felt like when I touched you?''

''Vaguely.'' Her hands began to tremble. Oh, how she'd missed this, this utter passion only Matt could make her feel. And it would be so easy to melt into his arms. She wanted it so badly she ached.

He slid his hands up, wetting her arms all the way to her shoulders, and turned her toward him. Dark and intense, his eyes locked on hers and she was helpless to look away. ''Remember the first time I kissed you?''

She gave a wobbly nod. Droplets of warm soapy water slid down her arms and dripped onto the kitchen floor.

"You tasted like chocolate. I wonder what you taste like tonight."

Probably her mother's chicken. And if it tasted as bad the second time around as it had the first, they were both in trouble.

Or they would cancel each other out.

In her mind, she kept telling herself to run. To get away. Unfortunately, her body wasn't responding. She knew he was going to kiss her. She *wanted* him to kiss her. And she didn't.

Where was rational Emily when she needed her?

Matt lowered his head and she held her breath, heart pounding in her chest. She felt hot and cold all at once. Frightened and excited.

In slow motion he moved closer and her head began to spin. She felt dizzy and breathless, then his lips brushed lightly over hers and everything inside her went liquid.

"Hmm, I remember this," he whispered against her lips.

She had to stop this. She had to come to her senses before someone walked in and saw them this way.

"I've been thinking," she said, easing away from him, thankful that he let her go. "I guess maybe we could try being friends again."

Something virile and primitive burned in his eyes. "Maybe that offer isn't on the table any longer. Maybe now I want more."

She backed toward the door. To hell with the dishes. Matt could finish them. She needed to get out of here before she did something monumentally stupid, like dragging him into the broom closet for a quickie. "You and I both know that would be a really bad idea."

"I don't know that, but I know how we can find out."

She stopped, her hand on the knob, her soapy fingers slipping on the brass. She recognized the determined look on Matt's face. Logically she knew this was destined to be a disaster, while her less logical side wanted everything he offered and more.

It was the "more" in that equation, and knowing he would never give it, that gave her the strength to open the door and walk out.

Matt watched Emily leave, knowing he'd won this round. He'd found her weakness—a way in.

She still wanted him.

When he'd touched her, she'd trembled. Actually *trembled*. He couldn't remember ever having that effect on a woman before. Well, not since the last time he'd been with Emily. That night on the beach they had both done their share of trembling. If she wanted him half as much as he wanted her, leaving tonight hadn't been easy. But this was Emily. She wouldn't give in to him without a fight. If he could build a multimillion dollar corporation from nothing, he could manage to seduce a woman. Even one as hardheaded as her.

And while they were busy fighting to see who would win this battle of wills, he would leave her boyfriend in the dust.

Ty had said to take this as far as necessary, and if this was his only angle, his only way in, he was going to take it. And if he was lucky, he and Emily would walk away from this as friends again. And he was going to enjoy himself.

Five

"**Y**ou want the guy," Alex said from his perch on the corner of Emily's desk. "Why won't you just admit it?"

Emily glared up at him, tired of having this identical conversation for two days running. What was it with everyone lately? Her mother had gotten on her case earlier that afternoon about spending time with Matt while he was in town. "We have to make him feel welcome," she'd said. Not an hour later Ty had called with a similar story, but he didn't possess the same air of subtlety as their mother. "He's rich, good-looking—what's not to like?" he'd asked.

It was like a freaking conspiracy.

She dropped her head in her hands, massaging away a killer headache in her temples. "I do not."

"But he's so *hot*. And rich." Alex grabbed a stack of messages off her desk. Messages Matt had left, that she hadn't yet returned because she was a big chicken. "And he's obviously interested."

"And he's leaving. I'm not looking to get my heart stomped on again. If you like him so much why don't *you* go out with him."

He let out a wistful sigh. "In my dreams, honey."

She gave him an eye roll. "Don't you have work to do?"

"You're awfully cranky for someone who claims not to need sex. I'm telling you, you'll feel so much better if you sleep with him then never call. Revenge is good for the soul."

If she thought it would make her feel better, she might just try it. But she didn't want revenge. She wanted to know what it was Matt wanted from her. One minute he said he wanted to be her friend, the next he was like a wolf on the prowl. And knowing she was his intended prey filled her with a sizzling sexual energy. That he could so effortlessly stir that reaction scared the hell out of her.

Her only defense was avoidance. So she wouldn't do something dumb, like fall in love with him again.

"If you insist on being so stubborn, how about dinner and a movie tonight instead? My treat. You've been working too hard."

Well, one of us has to, she wanted to say but held her tongue. Alex didn't mean to be irresponsible. He couldn't help that he was completely unfocused. "Only if we can see an action movie," she said. "No gushy romantic garbage."

He slipped off her desk. "You're on. I'll pick you up at six at your place."

"And no more talking about Matt?"

"Yes, fine. No more talking about Matt."

An evening when she wouldn't have to see Matt or think about Matt. It almost sounded too good to be true.

Matt pulled up in front of Emily's apartment, and parked. He'd had enough of being brushed off. Problems with the restaurant and office responsibilities had kept him tied up the last two days but now things were running relatively smoothly. This was his chance. This would be the night he would seduce Emily.

He walked up to her door and raised his hand to knock when he saw the note taped there inviting him in.

Well, it was inviting *someone* in, although he seriously doubted he was the intended receiver. Still, it did say to come in. And he didn't know for sure that it *wasn't* for him.

Feeling only slightly guilty, he stuffed the note in his pocket and opened the door, peering inside. From the bathroom, he heard the shower running.

Emily in the shower, water and soap sliding down her body. Naked and wet. His favorite combination.

This just kept getting better.

He stepped inside and closed the door, and as an afterthought locked it. For the briefest of moments he considered joining her in the shower, then wrote it off as a bad idea. Tempting, but unwise. When they took a shower together—and they would—it would be her idea.

Considering her reaction to him the other night in her parents' kitchen, finessing Emily into bed wouldn't really be all that difficult. He had decided, because he liked to continually present himself with new challenges, he wasn't going to make love to Emily until she asked for it.

Until then, he was predicting a fair amount of teasing and foreplay.

Her sofa bed was folded out, and since there was nowhere else to sit, he plopped down and stretched out lengthwise, stuffing a pillow under his head. He caught a hint of Emily's scent mingled with fabric softener and imagined her lying there. The sheets were a disheveled mess, as if she moved around a lot in her sleep. Unless her boyfriend was back and the sheets were messed up for an entirely different reason.

The thought stuck in his side like a thorn. He shouldn't feel this possessiveness toward her. Up until today, after repeated attempts to get in touch with her, he'd done a pretty good job of convincing himself he was only doing this for Ty and his parents. Yet with each unreturned call, his level of frustration had risen, until he could think of nothing but seeing her, of touching her again. One taste of her lips and he was like an addict, craving more.

He sighed and closed his eyes, exhausted beyond belief. He hadn't had a decent night's sleep since he'd gotten to Michigan. As hard as he'd tried to convince himself it was stress-related, or due to sleeping in an unfamiliar bed, odds were it had more to do with Emily. And when he *had* managed to catch a few hours of sleep, Emily had invaded his dreams. More often than not he'd woken aroused and restless and craving Emily's touch.

He stretched his arms over his head, sinking deeper into the mattress, feeling himself begin to drift off. And since a couple minutes of shut-eye wouldn't hurt, he didn't fight it. He had no idea how long he lay there and was only vaguely aware of the sound of a door opening, but he was too relaxed to move a muscle. Then something cold and wet hit him square in the chest and his eyes flew open.

Emily hovered over him. She wore a pair of cut-off shorts and a tank top the exact same silvery-blue as her eyes.

And she didn't look very happy to see him. "What the hell are you doing in my apartment?"

Matt grinned up at her. He grabbed the wet towel off his chest and tossed it back. "You invited me in."

She flung the towel onto the bathroom floor. "How? Telepathically?"

His grin widened and he pulled a slip of paper out of his pocket. "You left a note on the door for me."

She snatched it out of his hand and unfolded it. "This wasn't for you."

"It wasn't? Oops."

Oops my foot. He was far too amused for this to be anything but intentional. The man's ego knew no bounds.

She stomped over to the phone and punched in Alex's number, and when he answered said, "It's six-fifteen, why aren't you here?"

"And break up your little party? Not a chance, hon. I take it that note was for me?"

"You are *so* dead."

Emily peered out the front window and saw Alex's car parked across the street. He waggled his fingers at her.

"Trust me, Em, you need this."

There was a click and the line went dead. What

was this, screw-with-Emily's-life week? Was there anyone who *wasn't* trying to set her up with Matt?

"Stood up?" he asked. He was still lying on her bed, propped up on his elbows. And he looked damned good there.

"I don't suppose someone called and told you to come over here."

"Nope. Just my lucky night." He patted the spot next to him.

She spit out a rueful laugh. "You don't really think I'd get into bed with you?"

"I'll keep my hands to myself. Scout's honor."

She folded her arms over her chest. "Like I would be dumb enough to fall for that one again."

His smile widened, showing his dimples, and her resolve weakened the tiniest bit. "We'll call the bed the safe zone. No touching. I promise."

He might have been arrogant and occasionally sneaky, but when Matt made a promise, he didn't break it. She knew that without a doubt.

She crossed the room and dropped down next to him on the bed. He sat up beside her and nudged her with his shoulder. "Bad day?"

"You ever have one of those days when it feels like the entire world is against you?"

"At least once a week. Anything I can do to help?"

"You could go back to California."

He shrugged apologetically. "Sorry. You're stuck with me until the restaurant is finished. Would you settle for a back rub?"

"I can't, we're in the no-touching zone."

"Oh, yeah."

She gestured to his leg. "I keep meaning to ask, how's the knee? Does it ever give you trouble?"

"Occasionally," he said, rubbing a hand across the scars bracketing either side of his knee. "It aches sometimes when it rains, or if I push myself physically. I avoid contact sports and running."

"That must have been awful. To come so far in your career and then have it all snatched away."

"I was devastated," he admitted. "I felt like my life was over."

"I was watching the game when it happened. I saw you take the hit, the way they flipped you over, and I just knew you would be hurt. It was such a shock, seeing you lying there, your leg all twisted up." The memory made her shudder. "I can't imagine how much that must have hurt."

Matt nodded. "I'd taken a lot of hard hits in my years playing ball, had a couple of concussions, broken fingers, but I'd never felt pain like that."

"Right after it happened, my dad was on the phone with the airline. He didn't even know what hospital they were taking you to, but it didn't matter. My parents wanted to be there for you." Emotion stole up her throat. She laid a hand on his arm. "I should have been there, too. I've always felt that I let you down by not coming."

"God, Em, you didn't let me down." He covered her hand with his own, weaving his fingers through hers. "You didn't owe me anything."

She looked down at her their hands clasped together. This was the no-touching zone, but his hand felt too good, too soothing to pull away. "What are we doing here, Matt? Why is it I don't see you for years and now I can't get rid of you?"

He frowned, rubbing his thumb absently across the top of her hand. "I didn't plan any of this. I came back not knowing what would happen. I just knew I had to come."

"To reconnect?"

It was tough to explain something he didn't even understand. "Lately, I feel like something is missing in my life."

"You're rich, successful. To the world, it looks like you've got it all. What more could you possibly want?"

He shrugged. "Sometimes I wake up in the middle of the night in a cold sweat, gripped with this irrational fear that no matter how hard I work, no matter how much money I make, it will *never* be enough. I'll never be happy." He squeezed her hand and smiled. "But this is good—being here with you. I've really missed you, Em. When I leave this time, it will be as your friend. And I'm going to come back to visit. And you can come to visit me."

"I've always wondered, if I had just kept my feelings to myself, if we had never…maybe we would still be friends. I feel like I ruined everything."

"What happened is not your fault. We both wanted it."

"We did?"

A sick, cold feeling of dread slid through him. He'd always assumed what had happened was mutual. She'd sure as hell acted willing at the time. "Are you telling me I forced you?"

"No! Of course not. It was pretty obvious I wanted it. I just didn't know *you* did."

With a well of relief came a dash of confusion. "How could you not know?"

"I didn't hear from you after. I thought…" She pulled her hand from under his and tried to stand. "You know, we probably shouldn't be talking about this."

"Oh, no you don't." Matt grabbed her arm and pulled her back down next to him. "Talk to me, Emily."

She hesitated before she finally admitted, "I thought maybe you did it because you felt sorry for me."

He didn't know whether to feel insulted or dejected. "How could you think I would do that?"

"It was either that, or it was so bad you couldn't face me anymore." His eyebrow spiked and she added, "I'm sure it was obvious it was my first time. I had, like, zero experience. For all I know, I did everything wrong."

He buried his face in his hands and shook his head. Then his shoulders began to shake, and Emily realized he was *laughing.* Her blood heated to boiling, surging like fire through her veins. "You think this is funny?"

Laughing, he fell back against the mattress. "I think it's hilarious."

"You…you big stupid jock!" Did he have even the slightest clue how humiliating this was for her? Out of sheer frustration, she drove her fist into his gut, encountering only solid, rippling muscle. It was like trying to drive a Volkswagen through a Mack truck. He made a slight "oof" sound, but didn't stop laughing.

"I'm glad you think this is so amusing," she said, trying his biceps this time, giving new meaning to this-is-going-to-hurt-me-more-than-it-hurts-you. Pain radiated through her hand and up into her arm.

Remembering what she'd learned in her self-defense class, she pinched him just below his armpit.

Matt grabbed her wrist. "Ow! Damn it, that hurt."

Well, that had worked. He wasn't laughing at her anymore, only, now she couldn't move. She yanked hard against him. "Let go of me you big oaf."

"Hell, no, you're dangerous."

She pried at his fingers with her free hand, and before she had time to blink, he grabbed that wrist, too, flipped her over and pinned her to the bed. She gasped as the weight of his leg over both of hers trapped her against the mattress.

She struggled against his restraining hands. "Get off me, Conway."

Matt looked down at her, humor crinkling the corners of his eyes. "Not until you calm down."

She pushed up hard with her knee, and he countered the move by increasing the pressure of his leg, driving her deeper into the mattress. He was just too strong for her. Too darned big and heavy.

"We're in the no-touching zone," she said, pushing up against his hands.

"Listen to me, Emily. My not calling you had nothing to do with my lack of interest or your lack of experience. What we did that night was by far the single most erotic thing that's ever happened to me."

Emily stopped struggling and her anger leaked away. Her arms went slack against his restraining hands. "If you're just saying that to make me feel less stupid, I'll kill you."

"I wouldn't lie about something like that."

They were practically nose to nose, and the amusement she'd seen in Matt's eyes was gone. Now they were dark and intense. In response, she began to feel warm and heavy and boneless. Then that heat turned into an ache. An ache that settled itself between her thighs and tightened the peaks of her breasts into over-sensitized points. Definitely not the way one friend should be feeling about another friend.

"I'm not mad anymore," she said, thinking it was about time he let go of her, before they both did something stupid.

"Good," he replied, his eyes not leaving her face.

She glanced up at the hands still holding her firmly to the bed. "Maybe you should, um…move."

He shifted his leg between her two. His crisp leg hair chafed the sensitive skin of her inner thigh and she gasped at the intimate contact. As he rested his body firmly against her, she discovered she wasn't the only one feeling more than friendly.

"Is that what you had in mind?" he asked.

She wanted to arch against him. She wanted to take everything he was offering, but she knew it would be a mistake. And she knew if she didn't put an end to this soon, he would kiss her, and once he kissed her, she would be toast. "I'm not going to sleep with you, Matt."

He stared at her for several seconds, then he swore softly and let go of her hands. He rolled over onto the bed beside her and threw an arm over his eyes.

She sat up and poked him in the side. "You all right?"

"I will be in about five minutes. Sooner if you have a bucket of ice I could stick my head into."

The fact that he needed a bucket of ice after touching her sent a ridiculous little thrill through her. "'Fraid not."

Matt sighed deeply and sat up next to her. "You've changed, Emily. You're not the tough kid I left behind eleven years ago."

"I'm not?"

"Nope." He looked over at her, eyes full of sympathy. "You hit like a girl now."

The competitor in her rose up and crawled under her skin. Now he was really asking for it. "I may hit like a girl, but twenty bucks says I can still whoop your butt shooting hoops."

He gave her a wide grin, the thrill of the challenge clear on his face. "You're on."

Six

Matt leaned forward, resting his hands on his thighs, sucking hot, humid air into his lungs. The muscles in his legs were burning with exhaustion, his knee was on fire and sweat soaked his clothes, but he wasn't ready to give in yet. Not with Emily circling him, dribbling the basketball and looking as if she could go another ten rounds easy.

"Had enough?" she asked with a cocky grin.

He looked up at her, shading his eyes from the sun as it dipped below the trees bordering the park. "You're looking awfully pleased with yourself."

"For a wimpy girl, you mean? Why don't you just admit I'm better than you and give it up?"

"One more game," he said, pulling himself up and peeling his shirt over his head. "Double or nothing."

"You're already down a hundred and fifty dollars. You sure you want to take that kind of risk?"

"Hey, I'm playing with a handicap," he said, disgusted with himself for using his knee as an excuse for losing.

"So am I," she shot back. "I'm female."

Female or not, he'd forgotten how well she played. It probably didn't help that she still played regularly and he hadn't had his hands on a basketball since his injury. But he was determined to win just one more game.

He ducked past her, stealing the ball, and executed a flawless slam dunk. "First to ten points wins."

Twenty minutes later she made the winning shot, bringing the game to a slaughter of an end at ten to two.

Matt limped off the court, his pride mortally wounded, and collapsed on the blanket they'd spread out in the grass.

"Admit it," Emily said, dropping to her knees beside him. "I play pretty good for a girl."

"You play pretty good for a guy," Matt said, propping himself up on his elbows.

She took a long swallow out of her water then offered it to him. After he took a drink, she capped it and set it on the grass. "So, you didn't *let* me win, right?"

"*Let* you win? Emily, you eviscerated me."

"I just have a hard time believing you're that lousy. Not that you were ever that good at it, but at least it was marginally challenging."

He glared up at her. "Are you done gloating?"

She grinned and stretched out next to him on her side, propping her head in her hand, so they were face-to-face. Damn, she was pretty. If it were up to him, they would be lying this way in his bed back at the hotel. They would be naked and her skin would be flushed and moist not from basketball, but from hours of making love.

How she could think he hadn't enjoyed himself that night on the beach was beyond him. She'd been so aggressive, so sure of what she wanted, and so responsive to his every touch, every taste, he had wondered if it wasn't her first time after all. He'd been hurt that she hadn't told him when it happened. He'd thought she told him everything. And he'd wanted to find the guy who had stolen what should have been his and tear him limb from limb.

The thought of someone else's hands on her had burned him with jealousy. They'd been friends for years, and in all that time he'd barely given a physical relationship with her a second thought. That night he could think of nothing else. *He* wanted to be her first.

He still remembered how hot she'd felt as he'd entered her, how impossibly tight. Then he'd felt the barrier of her innocence give against his thrust, heard her sharp intake of breath, and he'd known she was his. It was as if the piece of him that had been missing had somehow slipped into place.

But it could never be more than one night. He had plans, dreams, and she didn't fit into them. In the morning they would go back to the way things had been. Back to being friends. It wasn't fair, and he knew he would probably hurt Emily, but it was just the way things had to be.

Then morning came, and all those feeling he'd experienced the night before, the need to be with Emily, hadn't burned away with the sunrise. In fact, it was worse. Everything he felt for her was still there, taunting him.

She would never know how difficult it had been to leave, or how close he'd been to giving it all up for her. Without the scholarship, he never would have been able to afford college. He *had* to go to UCLA. And without college ball, he never would have made it into the NFL. Had he not finished school and earned his degree, after his injury he would've had nothing to fall back on. He simply never had time for the kind of commitment Emily would have wanted. The one she deserved.

He still didn't.

"You're not what I expected," Emily said, her inquisitive blue eyes tugging Matt out of the past.

"What were you expecting?"

She shrugged. "I thought you would be more serious."

"I guess I am when I'm in California. More focused. I would never take time off to play one on one."

"How come?"

"Too busy. Weekdays I spend in the office, a couple evenings a week I stop in at the restaurant in L.A. to make an appearance. Every Sunday I fly to one of the other Touchdowns and spend a few hours."

"Every Sunday? Why?"

"It's good exposure and it draws the customers in."

"So when do you take a day off? When do you relax?"

He could barely recall the concept. "I don't. I have a condo in Cancun I've never been to. I own a villa in Italy I never have time to visit. If you want the honest truth, outside of work, I have no life.''

Her brow creased, as if the thought was a disturbing one. ''Then what's the point? Why work so hard if you can't enjoy what you've got?''

''When I figure that out I'll let you know.''

''So what about this Sunday? Which one are you going to?''

''This Sunday, I was supposed to fly to New York, but my plane is in for repairs.''

Her eyes widened. ''*Your* plane, as in the one you *own?*''

''It's a little plane,'' he said. ''A Lear.''

''Unless it's a model plane it's completely out of the realm of my comprehension. You can afford to buy a plane and you want even *more* money? When is it enough?''

He shrugged. He wished he knew. Although he had to admit, he'd felt different since he'd been back. He couldn't even put a finger on the exact emotion. Being with Emily again just felt…good. And not necessarily in a sexual way. He was just enjoying her companionship. Sitting here with Emily, he felt relaxed. Comfortable.

Content.

He couldn't remember the last time he'd felt that way. If only there were a way to capture it, to take it back to California with him.

''I always thought there would be this feeling I would get,'' he said. ''Then I would know that I'd made it, I'd succeeded. Then I could slow down and enjoy what I had. Maybe settle down and have a family. But lately, it seems like the harder I work, the further away the feeling gets.''

. "What does building a restaurant here have to do with it? Isn't it even more of a risk? Chapel isn't exactly a hoppin' place."

"I've proven myself in the business community, and had a decent, although short-lived career playing ball. I've resolved things with my parents to the point where I can forgive them and move on. The only thing I haven't done is prove I've made it to the people in Chapel."

"You know what I think?"

"Huh?"

"You spend way too much time worrying about what other people think."

She was probably right. In fact, he was sure she *was* right, but he'd run out of other options.

"You mentioned your parents. Do you see them very often?"

"As little as I have to."

"I heard you set them up in a pretty nice place in Florida."

Yeah, nice and far away, where he didn't have to watch them slowly committing suicide. "I used to think money would be the answer to their problems. I tried for a couple years to get them into detox programs, the best money could offer, but they never lasted for more than a week or two. There came a point where I had to back away. You can't save someone who doesn't want to be saved."

"At least you tried."

"I just make sure they're taken care of. If they're going to drink themselves to death, they'll do it in a nice condo on the beach. My mom has money to play bingo five nights a week and my father has his satellite dish and plasma TV to pass out in front of."

She reached over and rested her hand on his forearm. "They don't deserve you, Matt."

Something in the way she said his name and her gesture of comfort made the next words hard to say without emotion messing with his voice. "They weren't great parents, but they did the best they could."

The sympathy in her eyes nearly did him in. This was why he didn't like to talk to people about personal stuff. It did weird things to him, like turn him into a big wuss.

"So," he said, desperately needing a change of subject, "you haven't said much about your boyfriend. I take it it's not very serious."

"What makes you assume that? For all you know, we could be engaged."

"No ring."

She glanced down at the hand resting on his arm and something in her eyes darkened. He thought for sure she'd pull away, but she let it rest there. "I've never been real big into jewelry."

He reached up, rubbing her earlobe between his fingers. The look in her eyes went from dark to simmering. Don't fight it, he thought. You know you can't resist me. "No piercings."

"That's not exactly true," she said. "I do have one."

He examined her face, at all the obvious places, but didn't see any holes. "Let me guess, you had your navel done?"

She shook her head.

"Tongue?"

She made a face. "Yuck. No way."

"Where else is there?"

Her gaze wandered down to the front of her shirt. When he realized what she meant, all the air backed up in his lungs. "Your nipple?"

"It was purely an act of rebellion. In college, a friend of mine got hers pierced. My mom said if I ever did, she would disown me."

"So you did it anyway?"

A defiant grin spread across her face. "The next day."

"I guess she didn't disown you."

"I never told her. I ended up really liking it. Even though I was the only one who knew it was there, it made me feel…sexy. I'm pretty small up top, so it gives me that extra 'umph.'"

I'll bet, he thought, although from what he could see, she wasn't lacking in any particular area. He found his eyes riveted to her chest, curious whether he could see the outline through her clothing. "Doesn't it get caught on things?"

Her eyes lit with mischief, and something more. Something hot and teasing. "Actually, when you tug on it just a little or give it a twist, it's extremely erotic."

Matt swallowed hard to keep the excessive saliva from dribbling down his chin. He knew he wouldn't be satisfied until he was holding that ring in his teeth. "I've seen them in photos, but never in person."

Her eyebrow arched. "Are you asking if you can see mine?"

Hell, yes, he wanted to see it, but it wasn't so dark that the kids on the playground wouldn't notice if she lifted her shirt, or the group of teenagers playing volleyball several yards away wouldn't possibly see.

And he'd be damned if anyone was going to get a look at Emily's breasts. Anyone besides him, that is.

"This probably isn't the place," he said.

"Then maybe you'd like to see my tattoo instead?"

Nipple piercings *and* tattoos? "I'm afraid to ask where that is."

She shifted onto her back and unfastened her shorts and Matt's eyes just about fell out of his head.

"Uh, Emily?"

She rolled onto her stomach and lifted her shirt so that her lower back was exposed. "You'll have to pull my shorts down."

He sat up beside her and Emily watched, gratified by the hungry look in his eyes as he stared at her bare skin—the same look he'd had since she told him about her nipple. It made her feel desirable and powerful—something she hadn't felt in a very long time. Not since she'd given herself to him on the beach.

She was enjoying it far too much.

"Pull your shorts down?" he asked.

"Not all the way down. It's just below my waistline." She was playing with fire, but she couldn't seem to make herself stop.

He darted a glance around, as if he were afraid someone would see. Then he reached down and slipped two fingers under the waist of her shorts. The backs of his fingers caressed her skin as he eased the denim down, and gooseflesh broke out across her arms.

A breath escaped him in the form of a sigh. "What is it?"

She looked back over her shoulder at him. "An orchid. My favorite flower."

"The detail is amazing." He pulled her shorts lower, to see the entire yellow flower blooming across the lowest part of her back and the very top of her buttocks. As if he were touching the living specimen, he brushed a thumb across the delicate petals. That frustrating ache burned to life low and deep inside her.

"No tan line," he said, but it came out sounding more like a growl.

"It shows up best against tanned skin."

"I'm not even going to ask how you managed that." Matt flattened his palm against her, his large hand encompassing her entire lower back. "I think I want to see the nipple ring now."

"I think that would be a bad idea."

He slipped his hand down her side, his fingers just inside the waist of her shorts, which were already several inches lower than they should have been. His hand traveled slowly up her side, lightly tracing each of her ribs, all the way up to the edge of her bra. She closed her eyes and curled her fingers into the blanket. The ache was now a throb as need overwhelmed her and blood raced through her veins.

She rolled onto her side and looked up at him. His eyes were dark with desire. "I'm not going to sle—"

Before she could finish the sentence, Matt lowered his head and pressed his lips to hers. The sizzling reaction was instantaneous. She was lost.

It began slow and sweet, his lips brushing oh-so-gently. She felt herself go weak under the tender pressure of his mouth. Very lightly, he traced her lower lip with the tip of his tongue. When she touched her tongue to his, the grip on her side tightened and his fingers pressed deep into her flesh, sending shocks of sensation through her stomach. He tasted exactly as he had eleven years ago. He smelled the same and his hands felt just as good against her skin. And now that she'd had a taste of him, a sample of what he could give her, she was having a hard time putting on the brakes. Of course, with Matt kissing her senseless, she wasn't using a lot of brain power.

Somewhere in the back of her mind she knew they were in a public park, but she also knew it was growing darker by the minute. Families were packing up and clearing out. Teenagers gathered in packs around picnic tables, others hung out in the wooded areas most likely doing exactly what she and Matt were doing. No one was paying attention to the couple on the blanket.

Just for a few minutes, she promised herself. Then I'll stop him. But those few minutes passed too quickly, so she decided to give it just a few minutes more.

Matt flattened his hand over her stomach, dipping inside her open shorts to the very tops of her bikini underwear, and she froze.

He must have sensed her apprehension because he went very still above her.

"Matt, I—"

"I know," he growled, rolling away and sprawling out flat on the blanket. "You're not going to sleep with me."

Seven

Matt stabbed the off button on his cell phone and repressed the urge to chuck it at the nearest brick wall. Construction on Touchdown was officially shut down.

Apparently, Eric Dixon had a little more clout than Matt had anticipated. His lawyer was pressing for a lawsuit, but the last thing Matt needed was a long drawn-out legal battle. It wouldn't exactly endear the people of the city to the idea of eating at his restaurant.

And every day the building sat there deserted, he lost more money. Not to mention that until it was finished, he would be stuck in this godforsaken city, where more than a few people had made it clear he was no longer welcome.

Late last night someone had spray-painted derogatory comments and a few colorful expletives across the exterior of the restaurant and the construction trailer. The police promised to increase future nightly patrols of the area, but were already making noise like there was little chance of catching the responsible party. And though he'd hired a painter to cover the evidence, he couldn't erase the foul image from his mind.

He watched as the construction crew cleared out their equipment. They had other jobs to occupy their time while he worked something out. Eric had approached Matt earlier in the morning offering a monetary solution. One that would cost Matt in the neighborhood of six figures. If only he'd had a tape recorder handy to nail the sleazy bastard.

Matt already knew what he needed to do. He had a solution. He just had to take that step. Emily's parents had done so much for him already, he didn't know how to ask what would be his final favor.

Then he would win.

He flipped his phone open and dialed Emily's father at his engineering firm. He was told by the secretary that Mr. Douglas would be out of the office all week. Matt tried him at home next, but got the answering machine, so he called Ty.

"They drove up to Saugatuck to stay with friends," Ty told him. "They're due back next Thursday or Friday, I think."

A full week. Damn.

Matt hung up, cursing himself for waiting. If he'd known Mr. and Mrs. Douglas were going out of town he would have approached them before they left. If they had agreed to his terms he could have at least gotten the ball rolling. He'd have lost maybe a week, now he was looking at two or three.

Which meant he had that much more time to sit around and twiddle his thumbs. He could always go back to L.A., but his plane was still awaiting a part and the thought of taking a flight on a commercial airline held about as much appeal as a bikini wax—which he'd never actually had, but they sure as hell didn't look like much fun to him. And oddly enough, he didn't want to go back to L.A. He didn't feel like working, which for him was like saying he didn't feel like breathing.

The thought of sitting in his office, submerged in a mountain of paperwork his staff could just as easily handle without him made Matt feel restless. Anything important that needed going over he could do through e-mail or fax and anything that needed signing would reach him overnight via Fed Ex. Meetings he could handle through conference calls. The office ran just fine without him, and that had him wondering why it was he spent so damned much time there.

On the positive side, time off from work meant more time to seduce Emily. The memory of her skin, her scent, the taste of her lips was driving him nuts. And he hadn't been able to stop thinking about that nipple ring. Though it was a slow process, last night he'd made some serious headway. If he'd been insistent, he probably could have taken it even further, but what was the fun in that? When the time was right, she would be begging for it. Then he would finally get to do everything he hadn't done that night on the beach. Which, come to think of it, wasn't much.

The question now was, what would his next move be? With all this time on his hands, what was he supposed to do with himself?

As the last truck pulled out of the lot, Matt took a final look at the building and smiled, knowing exactly what he needed to do.

"Hey."

Emily looked up from her computer screen, her traitorous heart fluttering at the sight of Matt standing in her office doorway looking tanned and healthy and way too gorgeous for his own good—or hers. "Hey. What's up?"

"I came to talk about work."

"Okay." She tried to keep her tone light when in reality her heart was sinking. He was probably here to tell her that they'd lost the contract to another nursery. Maybe sleeping with him had been a condition of the job.

As the thought formed she knew it was completely unfair. She'd been the aggressor last night, the one to bring up the nipple ring, to take down her pants and show him her tattoo. She still didn't know what had gotten into her. Maybe it was the way Matt looked at her as though she was the only woman on the planet. He made her feel so desirable and, well…feminine. She hadn't realized how much she'd missed that.

She'd pretty much given up on men—at least for now. As far as she could figure, they felt threatened by her independence. Most men seemed to like a woman they could coddle and take care of. Someone gentle and delicate that they could put up on a pedestal. Not one who could run circles around them on the basketball court, or recite from memory the stats from the Detroit Red Wings entire last season. She didn't wear makeup, didn't own a dress—nor did she plan to purchase one—and pantyhose gave her a rash. At five feet nine inches, high-heeled shoes put her at eye level with most men she knew, and several inches above others. Which is why she didn't own any of those either.

Alex loved her for the person inside. He was her best friend, her confidant. He had great taste in clothes and even better taste in men. Unfortunately, being friends with a gay man didn't do much for a girl's ego.

When Matt looked at her—very much the way he was looking at her now—she felt like a woman.

Matt stepped into her office and sank into the chair across from her desk. "I've run into a bit of a snag with the building inspector. Construction has been put on hold. I just wanted to let you know there's no rush getting that bid to me."

Which meant her commission would come later, and her shop was that much further away. Swell. "Thanks for the heads up."

"Instead of flying back to L.A. while my lawyers work this out, I thought I might take a couple of days off. Maybe go fishing."

"What, like a vacation?"

"Yeah, I figure I'm due."

Emily narrowed her eyes at him. "Who are you and what have you done with Matt?"

He grinned. "I want you to come with me. Can you get a couple of days off?"

Before she could say no, Alex appeared in the doorway. "Of course Emily could get a couple days off."

He breezed in, a hand stretched to Matt in greeting. His hair, as always, was perfect, his clothes spotless and his manners impeccable. And he could play the man's man role to a T. "You must be the infamous Matt Conway."

Matt stood and shook Alex's hand, looking to Emily for an explanation.

"Matt, this is Alex Marlette."

"A pleasure," Alex said, pumping Matt's hand. "What's this about Emily needing a few days off?"

"I don't," she told Alex. "I have too much to do here."

Alex dropped Matt's hand and turned to her. "I had my vacation. It's only fair you get some time off, too. Where did you plan to take her, Matt?"

Matt looked hesitant to answer, as if maybe this was some sort of trick question. "Um, fishing?"

"Emily loves to fish. Of course she'll go."

"But the accountant is coming," Emily told Alex. "We need to go over the books."

Alex turned to Matt. "I'm sorry, could you give us a minute alone?"

"I'll wait out front," Matt said, looking back and forth between the two of them as if they were both more than a little weird.

He had no idea.

When he was gone, Alex turned to her, fanning his face, slipping easily back into his typical, flaming self. "Whoa. Talk about steamy."

"I'm not leaving."

"This is your big chance."

"To do what? Screw up my life?"

"Em, honey, this self-imposed celibacy thing you've got going is getting really old. Take a couple of days and have fun."

"There is no self-imposed celibacy. I just haven't

met anyone I've wanted to sleep with.'' If he only knew how close she'd been to doing exactly that last night.

Emily rubbed her eyes with a thumb and forefinger. She was exhausted after one very long, sleepless night. In just a few days her prudently managed life had been propelled into chaos and Alex was asking her to make it even worse. ''I can't just pick up and leave. I have responsibilities.''

''It'll all be here when you get back.'' He grabbed her arm and physically hauled her from the chair. ''If you don't go I'm going to fire you. Then you'll never get the money together for your shop. I swear I'll do it.''

''You would not. This place would fall apart without me.''

''Honey, you give yourself far too much credit. I'm not completely incapable.''

''Yes, you are.''

The insult slid right off his back. ''I'll pay you time and a half for your vacation days.''

That one stopped her. She did a mental calculation of how much money that would be. ''Seriously? You would actually *pay* me to go on vacation? For the whole weekend?''

''I would, now will you go?''

''Is there something you're not telling me?''

''Yes, you're a major pain in the butt. Just go and have fun.''

Honestly, the idea of a couple days away from the nursery sounded like heaven. She couldn't recall the last time she'd taken a vacation. She'd been too focused on raising the money for her shop, on keeping the business running smoothly. How much damage could Alex possibly do?

On second thought, she didn't even want to go there. "What about the accountant? We have to get ready for the audit."

"I can handle it. I'm really not as incompetent as you like to think."

"Maybe I don't want to go with him. Did that ever occur to you?"

"You need closure, hon. As much as you refuse to admit it, after all these years, you still have a thing for the guy."

"Says who?"

"Says you, every time I catch you looking at his picture in a magazine, or watching a clip about him on the news. You get that sappy, sad, faraway look and you swoon all over the place."

She snorted. "I've never swooned in my life."

"When was the last time you were on a date? Or had a relationship? Or *sex?* You do remember what that is?"

Emily gave up the battle and allowed him to shove her out the office door. "I'll get paid time and a half? Even though the nursery is barely hanging on?"

"I'll take it out of my salary."

"For how long?"

He glanced at the calendar on her desk. "Today is Thursday? I don't want to see you back here until Monday morning."

"You promise you're not just saying this to get rid of me?"

"I promise."

She hesitated. "I don't know…"

Alex lowered his voice. "Okay, how about this.

Take some time off or I'll tell your parents we're not really dating.''

She knew exactly what that meant; her parents trying to set her up with every available single man in the city. Anything to get themselves a tribe of grandchildren. She narrowed her eyes at him. "You wouldn't."

"Try me." He slammed and locked the door before she could reply to his threat. It looked as if she would be taking a few vacation days. That didn't mean she would be spending them with Matt.

He was in the parking lot waiting for her, leaning against the back of his SUV, arms folded across his chest. The sun glinted off his dark hair and made his skin look golden. As usual, the sight of him accelerated her heartbeat and punched up her hormone level several notches.

This was not good. After what had almost happened last night in the park, a fishing trip with Matt would be a very bad idea.

"Did your boyfriend really just encourage you to go away on vacation with me?" he asked.

"That doesn't mean I'm going." She pulled out her keys and headed for the company truck.

He fell in step beside her. "He's a nice guy."

"You sound surprised. Did you think I wouldn't be able to attract someone nice?"

"You know that's not what I meant. If you were my girlfriend, no way in hell would you be going away anywhere with anyone but me."

The passion with which he made the statement alarmed and thrilled Emily at the same time. What would it be like to be Matt's girlfriend? To be his wife? To have homes all over the world. To own expensive cars and clothes and have a plane at their disposal.

Lonely.

It would be unbearably lonely. The hours he worked, it would be like living with a ghost. No amount of wealth would be worth that. If he were penniless and worked a nine-to-five job he would be a better catch as far as she was concerned.

Besides, she didn't have the time to invest in a relationship either. Like Matt, she enjoyed the challenge of earning what she wanted. She would feel the pride that shone like a prize in his eyes when he talked of his accomplishments. It's what she had waited her whole life for. True independence.

If she were to marry Matt, on the entirely remote chance that he ever asked, along with the wealth and prestige, she would feel like a sellout. Where would the challenge be?

If the business didn't take off as she hoped, she would be disappointed, but at least she could say she'd tried, she'd given it one hundred percent. On her own.

When they reached the truck Matt stepped ahead of her, blocking the door. "Come with me," he said. "We'll have fun. We can go anywhere in the world you want."

"Alex may be trusting, but I know you too well, Conway. You want to get me away from here so you can get me into bed."

"Not true," he said, and at her look of complete disbelief, added, "Not *entirely* true. I'd just like to spend time with you."

She would love to go away with him. But not if

this was some quest to soften her up. She didn't know if she had the strength to fight it anymore.

God, she was having trouble remembering *why* she was fighting it.

Oh yeah, because she would fall in love with him again, and he would leave, and she would be devastated.

"Can you promise that you will not under any circumstances try to seduce me?" she asked. "Promise that this vacation will be one hundred percent platonic."

When he didn't answer, disappointment burned deep. At least he was honest. He could very easily lie to get what he wanted, but that wasn't Matt's style. If things were different, if they both had very different lives, they might have been good together.

And they both knew it.

He seemed to realize it was a lost cause, and stepped away from the door. It wasn't like him to give up so easily and she felt equal parts relieved and disappointed. She climbed in and started the engine.

He leaned in the open window. "Think about it. If you change your mind, call my cell phone."

Because he looked so hopeful, and completely irresistible, she leaned over and pressed a kiss to his cheek before she drove away.

Emily climbed out of the truck and stretched her stiff limbs, inhaling the earthy scents of pine and moss and feeling an odd mix of emotions—the way she always felt when she came up to her parents' cottage. She relished the peace that came with submersing herself in nature, yet this place held so many memories. Some full of laughter and fun, others bittersweet. She'd experienced the best and worst times of her life here.

The best, when Matt had made love to her on the beach, the worst when she woke the following morning, her heart swelled to capacity, only to have a "talk." She'd been back dozens of times since, and still experienced that sense of loss. Maybe it would never go away.

She grabbed her things from the front seat and let herself into the cottage. Exhausted from the three-hour drive, she tossed her bag in her bedroom to unpack later. Right now she was going to take advantage of the last few hours of afternoon sun and lie out on the beach. Later she would go into town and buy a few supplies.

Alone, a voice echoed in her head.

Yeah, so what. It wouldn't be the first time she'd come here alone, and it probably wouldn't be the last.

And what, that was supposed to make her feel better?

She peeled her clothes off, fighting a wave of loneliness despite her internal pep talk. She couldn't help wondering what Matt was up to. Where had he gone? His villa in Italy? His condo in Cancun? And who was he with? Had he found someone else to keep him company? Someone willing to do what Emily wasn't?

She tried to convince herself she didn't care, but that didn't take away the sick feeling in the pit of her stomach. What an impossible situation. Two people who were hopelessly attracted and completely wrong for each other.

She wrapped herself in a beach blanket, slipped her sandals on, and headed outside. She followed the narrow trail through the trees and down to the lake. As she emerged from the dense foliage onto the sandy cove, sunshine wrapped around her, warming her bare arms and shoulders. With her father semi-retired, her parents came up regularly during the summer months, sometimes for weeks at a time. The boat was parked in the slip next to the dock, and she was sure there were sodas and beer in the fridge. The freezer would be stocked with steaks and burgers ready to barbecue.

Emily kicked off her sandals and dug her toes into the hot sand. Though their own stretch of beach was secluded and private, the lake was alive with activity. Jet Skis and motor boats cut foamy paths through the water. The playful shouts of children swimming and splashing traveled on the breeze.

Emily knelt down in the sand and unfolded herself from the blanket. Boats rarely ventured so close that someone would see she was naked. And if one did, she would hear its engine and have plenty of time to cover herself.

She stretched out on her stomach, her gaze drawn to the fire pit, to the spot where Matt had made love to her. She felt that familiar pull of longing.

Even though it had been her first time, and she'd heard countless horror stories about the pain, she hadn't been the least bit afraid. She'd spent more hours than she could count daydreaming about that moment. Wishing for it with all of her heart. She couldn't have been more ready and Matt had been unbelievably sweet and gentle with her. It might have been her imagination, or maybe just wishful thinking, but at the time she could have sworn he'd been nervous. Matt, who was rumored to have scored with dozens of girls.

The second time had been different. She'd been even bolder and he'd been much more aggressive. Not rough, but not exactly gentle either. He was suddenly the Matt she'd heard rumors about in the girls' locker room. The one who knew exactly what to do to drive a girl crazy. He'd touched her in ways that to this day made her feel that same hot restlessness in her limbs. A deep longing, an ache no one else had been able to relieve.

By the third time, she'd chucked the last of her inhibitions. Her only goal had been to give him the same bone-deep satisfaction he'd made her feel. When the fire died and they'd gone back to the cottage, there had been very little left unexplored. They knew each other more intimately than she thought two people could. She had lain in bed afterward, reliving it all in her head, committing each second to memory.

She thought she'd gotten over him. Now that he was back, she wasn't sure what to feel anymore. He wanted to be friends. He wanted her to visit him in California.

And he wanted sex.

And heaven knows, so did she. Maybe she was being silly telling him no. They were both consenting adults. What was she proving, staying up here at the cottage all by herself? That she could manage on her own? She already knew that. She'd been doing it for years. For *too* long.

As if she'd conjured him up by sheer will alone, Emily heard the low rumble of Matt's voice behind her.

''Now I see why you don't have tan lines.''

Eight

Matt watched as Emily shrieked in surprise and yanked the edges of the blanket around herself. She needn't have bothered. He'd been standing there long enough to see everything. And a little longer to commit it all to memory. Now that he'd seen all of that gloriously tanned and flawless skin, his desire for her had multiplied to an aching need. A need not only to lay her out beneath him and bury himself deep inside her, but to feel that closeness, that connection he'd felt only with her.

"What the hell are you doing here, Conway?"

He flashed her a wide grin. "Fishing."

She tucked the blanket tightly around herself and rose to her feet. "You *followed* me?"

"Look me in the eye and tell me you're not happy to see me. That you wanted to stay up here all by yourself."

She shoved her feet into her sandals and stomped past him. "That's not the point."

On the contrary, that was exactly the point.

He followed her through the woods to the cottage, a grin on his face. He'd seen the flash of excitement when she'd first turned around. She was happy to see him, and trying awfully hard to hide it. "I didn't have to follow you. I knew you would come here."

"How could you possibly know that?"

"It was the first place I thought of, too."

There was the slightest hesitation in her step, and he knew his words had hit their mark. He followed her into the cottage and to her bedroom. He leaned in the doorway while she rummaged through a duffel bag for clothes, reminded of one of the things he'd always liked about her. She could throw a couple of days' worth of clothes together in less than ten minutes and didn't need a ten-piece set of luggage to carry it all. He'd never dated a woman who wasn't severely high-maintenance. Even in high school. It had him wondering what it was about him that attracted that kind of woman. And what it was about that kind of woman that he found attractive, because honestly, the luggage thing really annoyed him.

It occurred to him that Emily was the complete opposite of everything he normally looked for in a woman. Which made him wonder if he wasn't deliberately dating women he knew would irritate him.

"If you're only here to get me into bed, you might as well leave right now," she said, her back to him.

"I told you before, I want us to be friends. When I leave Michigan, I want us to continue that friendship." Why was it every time he thought about going back to L.A.—his home—he felt utterly empty?

She turned to him, eyes scrutinizing. "So, you're saying you no longer want to get me into bed?"

"Do I want you, Em? Yeah, I do. But if friendship is all you can give me right now, that will have to be enough." He took a step toward her, but hung back just far enough so the move wouldn't come off as overtly sexual. He wished she'd drop the blanket so he could see that nipple ring. It was all he'd thought about on the way up.

"Let me stay, Em."

"You promise you won't try to get me into bed?"

He could be wrong, but he had the distinct feeling that by saying "bed," she was leaving open a hell of a lot of options. Or was he letting his imagination get the best of him?

"I promise."

For a long moment she only stared at him, and finally she said, "We'll need supplies. We'll have to go into town for groceries and bait."

She was letting him stay. A slow grin spread across his face. She was as good as his.

She just didn't know it yet.

Matt followed Emily down the aisle of the country market in town. Talk about a blast from the past. A typical mom-and-pop establishment, little had changed in here in the last decade. And while it still boasted decor reminiscent of the Brady era, it was clean and the selection surprisingly diverse for its remote location.

And like so many other things pertaining to his past, he'd missed it more than he realized.

"We should get cereal for breakfast," Emily said,

swiping a box of Kangaroo Crunch off the store shelf.

Matt took the box from her and read the nutritional chart. "Do you know how much sugar is in this?"

"Well, yeah, that's kind of the point. How else am I going to wake up at four in the morning?" She grabbed a package of iced pastries and tossed those in the cart as well.

"You mean women actually eat this stuff? I thought all you ate was lettuce and tofu."

Emily shrugged. "I have big hips and no diet in the world is going to change that. I may as well enjoy eating."

"Emily, do you know what I find most appealing about you? The fact that you actually have hips. You have meat on your bones." At the odd look she gave him, he added, "That's a compliment."

"I wasn't sure."

She really didn't have a clue how attractive she was. She had no idea how tough it was to stand within a few feet and not touch her, not undress her with his eyes. He was trying really hard not to do anything blatantly sexual. He didn't want to do anything to scare her off. But, damn, it was hard not to touch her.

Take it slow, he reminded himself.

"Believe it or not," he said, "I'm tired of dating women who look as though a strong breeze could knock them over. The kind who excuse themselves to the rest room to throw up after every meal."

She gave him a "yeah, right" look.

"I'm serious. I've taken women out to dinners in five-star restaurants, where you can drop three or four hundred easy on dinner. Double that if they want champagne. There's a reason they're trotting off to the john between every course. I once dated a model who actually excused herself to throw up after dinner.''

Emily made a face. "Yuck. You run with an interesting crowd, Conway.''

"I don't exactly run with anyone. They just kind of…attach themselves to me.''

Emily grabbed a loaf of wheat bread from the shelf—the first healthy thing she'd picked up. "People respect you. They want to be around you.''

"They respect who they think I am.''

"How do you expect them to see you for who you really are unless you let them?''

"And what if, when I let them see the real me, they aren't so impressed anymore?'' He winced at his own words. That didn't come out the way he'd meant it to.

A slow smile spread across Emily's face. "I'll be damned. He is still in there.''

"Who?''

"The Matt I knew when we were kids. The one who looked self-confident, like he owned the world, but on the inside felt like he never quite measured up.''

Her words stunned him.

She was wrong. He simply valued his privacy and was particular about who he let into his life. He'd left those insecurities behind when he left Michigan.

Hadn't he?

"It's okay,'' she said. "I liked the old Matt.''

Troubled by her words, Matt followed behind her as she picked out packaged lunch meat and cheese, then onto the register where she added half a dozen chocolate bars to the cart.

"That should about cover it," she said, as the cashier rang it all up.

Matt pulled out his wallet.

"I'll get this," she said.

"The hell you will. It goes against the natural order of the sexes. The man pays for the food."

She rolled her eyes. "Spare me the sexist bull, Conway."

"Sexist bull or not, it's the way I do things."

Emily frowned. "I don't like the idea of you buying me stuff."

"Yeah, well I don't like you buying me stuff either."

The cashier looked back and forth between them as if they were seriously disturbed. "Someone has to pay for it."

"We could share the cost," Emily reasoned.

"Yeah, okay," he agreed, because he was pretty sure arguing would get him nowhere. She was struggling to make ends meet, yet she still wouldn't let him pay for the damned food. She was definitely unlike any woman he'd ever dated. He found himself appreciating that fact more every minute he spent with her.

They split the cost of the groceries, packed it in the truck and headed back to the lake. He steered the truck back down the long, tree-lined dirt lane. He'd been there so many times in his youth he could have driven blindfolded. The log-cabin-style cottage, tucked deep into the woods, looked exactly as it had when they were kids. Beyond the cabin he could see glimpses of shimmering blue lake between the trees.

The scent of pine and earth and the warm breeze rustling the leaves greeted him like a long-lost friend. That it felt so good to be back surprised him. He'd missed so many things about his old life, but hadn't realized it until he'd come home.

"We should load the fishing supplies into the boat today so we can get an early start in the morning," Emily said as they carried the groceries in.

"Is it all still in the shed out back?"

"Should be."

"You put the groceries away, I'll take care of the fishing stuff."

She propped a hand on one hip. "Let me guess. Putting groceries away is women's work?"

He flashed her an easy smile, one that said she'd hit the nail on the head, and headed out the door. His ideas were borderline chauvinist, yet she couldn't muster a bit of anger. Men typically saw her as one of the guys and treated her accordingly. They didn't open doors, or pay for meals. And they sure as hell didn't look at her as though they wanted to rip her clothes off and ravage her—the way Matt had been looking at her on the beach. Of course, she hadn't had any clothes to rip off, had she?

He didn't seem to notice that she was about as far from supermodel material as a girl could get. Yet there was no question, their desire was mutual. But for how long? Should this ever progress past a brief fling, if say, he asked her to go back to California with him, one day he was going to look at her and realize she was all wrong. He would have some fancy event he would want to take her to and discover she wasn't, and never would be, arm-dressing.

Besides, she thought as she put the last of the groceries away, she didn't want to leave Michigan. She had plans. Her family and friends were here. It was home to her. She wasn't sure she could give that up for anyone. Not even Matt. Not anymore.

She headed outside and down to the beach. Matt was still on the boat, so she waded out calf-deep into the water, feeling inexplicably sad. Why, when a relationship was destined to fail, did she still yearn for it?

"Is the water cold?"

Emily turned to see Matt walking across the sand toward her. "Not too cold."

He kicked his sandals off and waded into the water beside her. "Everything looks the same."

She gazed around. Nothing ever seemed to change up here, yet everything was different this time.

"You okay?" he asked.

"Yeah," she lied. Well, it wasn't a complete lie. She was only slightly not okay. "Why?"

He tucked his hands in his pockets and shrugged. "You had kind of a funny look on your face. You looked…sad, I guess."

Her attention naturally strayed to the fire pit, and he followed with his own eyes.

"Having regrets?" he asked.

"There's nothing about that night I regret, Matt. Do you regret it?"

How could he regret the most amazing experience of his life? How could he regret connecting, bonding so deeply with another person? "Never. I just regret that I hurt you."

She nodded. "Yeah, that part did suck."

"Maybe someday, in a couple of years, when things settle down for me…"

"Be still my heart." She clasped a hand to her breast and adopted a horrible Southern drawl. "I shall wait till the end of time for you to return."

"Too much to ask, huh?" Kind of like having his cake and eating it, too. As he'd reminded himself so many times over the years, she deserved better. "Is it because of Alex?"

"Alex is very special."

The next words were almost impossible for him to squeeze out. "Do you love him?"

Her foot swung like a pendulum through the surf. "He's my best friend. He keeps me sane."

Jealousy twisted him in knots. Even worse than the thought of Emily having an intimate relationship with someone else was the thought that he'd been replaced as her best friend. He wanted to fill that spot. He wanted it so badly it was painful. Maybe she just didn't have room for him in her life anymore.

Well, dammit, she would have to make room, because he wanted back in, and he wasn't taking no for an answer. He *needed* her. He was no longer doing this for Emily's family. Or even for Emily. This was all about him, what *he* wanted.

Now all he had to do was figure out exactly what that was.

"Why don't we put on our suits and go swimming before we make dinner?" she said, obviously ready for a conversation change.

"Who needs suits?" Matt said. He peeled his shirt off and tossed it onto the sand. Emily's eyes widened, as if she thought he might strip down naked right in front of her. He would if that's what she wanted. "We can wear our clothes."

"Our clothes?"

"I remember you used to love jumping off the dock in your clothes."

"Conway, the only time I ever went off the dock in my clothes is when you threw me—" Recognition darkened her eyes and she began to back away from him, onto the sand. "You wouldn't."

With an evil grin, he began to mirror her steps. "What kind of vacation would this be if I didn't throw you off the dock, Emily? It's tradition."

"That's one tradition I can do without, thank you." She turned and started to run, and while she was damned fast, even with a bum knee he was faster. With little effort he caught up to her. He hooked an arm around her waist and swooped her lithe form up and over his shoulder.

She screamed and kicked but was laughing too hard to put up much of a fight, as she had when they were kids. "Let me go, Conway!"

If he'd heard an ounce of conviction in her words he would have put her down. Instead he wrapped an arm across her lush behind and tucked her firmly against him. He'd held her this way half a dozen times a year throughout the better part of his childhood, but he couldn't remember it ever feeling this nice. Or having the urge to slide his hand across her firm rear end, between her silky thighs...

"You big dumb jock, let go of me!" she screamed through another fit of laughter.

Ignoring her pleas, he trudged through the sand and down the length of the dock.

She beat at his back with her fists. "You are so dead, Conway. When you least expect it, I'll get my revenge."

"I'm pretty scared," he said, and his mild tone said he was anything but. He reached the end of the dock and, with beautiful execution and no hesitation, tossed her into the lake. She landed with an enormous splash and disappeared under the water.

He crouched down, waiting for her to surface. When she didn't he felt a sliver of concern and immediately dismissed it. She'd been on the swim team in high school. If he knew Emily, she was hiding under the dock, waiting for just the right moment to reach up and pull him into the water.

He sat back a little, just in case.

"I know what you're up to and I'm not falling for it," he called into the water. The words were barely out of his mouth when a shadow passed across him from behind, and he felt a wet hand planted firmly on his back. He looked up to see two perfectly formed breasts with small, dark, erect peaks under a soaked, transparent tank top. And, *aw hell,* the outline of one enticing nipple ring. Then he crashed headfirst into the water.

Matt picked his cell phone up from the picnic table where he'd set it out to dry, feeling an eerie sense of panic. The cottage had no phone, and without a phone line he had no Internet hookup. And Emily, to his disbelief, didn't have a cellular. He'd thought that in this day and age everyone had a mobile phone, or at least a pager.

He was, in essence, completely cut off from the outside world. It felt unnatural, as if one of his limbs had been amputated.

Talk about a wake-up call. There was something

seriously wrong with him if he couldn't survive three days without a cell phone.

"Is it dry yet?" Emily asked as she cleared away the paper plates and plastic cutlery from their dinner. The distress in her voice was more than clear. She felt pretty bad for what she'd done, regardless of how many times he'd told her it was okay. If anyone was at fault, it was him. If he hadn't tossed her in the lake, she never would have retaliated by pushing him in. And if not for the lake he never would have gotten a glimpse of that nipple ring. It was worth the hours of sexual torture he'd endured while he imagined what it would be like to take that tiny ring between his teeth and give it a tug.

The torture of not being able to get hold of his secretary was far worse.

"Maybe you should try turning it on," she said.

"It's only been a couple of hours." He set it back down, resisting the urge to dial his voice mail. "If I turn it on wet, I'll completely fry the circuits."

"I'm really sorry, Matt. If I had known you were wearing your phone—"

"I told you before, it's not your fault."

"If there's any way I can make it up to you."

Oh, man, how often did a guy get an offer like that? Where should he start? Several ways instantly sprang to mind, but he was pretty sure the things he was thinking weren't exactly what she was thinking. Most involved his mouth on various parts of her anatomy.

Just the thought caused a tightening in his groin.

He gazed at her mouth, his lips tingling in anticipation, not to mention the other parts of him that had begun to tingle as well. He needed to get some blood flowing back to his brain. He had to keep his focus.

"If it's ruined I'll replace it. Just let me know how much."

"The cost isn't important," he said.

"You're worried about work. About your office not being able to get a hold of you."

Not just the office, but he'd left a message with Emily's parents asking them to call as soon as possible. The sooner he talked to them, the sooner he could get construction up and running. He hoped.

"You can go back," she said. "If you leave right now you would make it to Chapel by about 1:00 a.m."

At the mere thought of completely abandoning his business, apprehension gripped his stomach. Sweat beaded his brow and trickled down the side of his face. He was in worse trouble than he'd thought if the idea of a few days away from work triggered a panic attack. Had he chained himself so completely to his company that he'd become obsessed?

It ended here, dammit. Maybe it was time he reevaluated his priorities. Maybe it was time he started to live a little. He'd promised himself a vacation and if that meant cutting himself off from the world, he'd try like hell to relax and have a good time.

"No," he told Emily. "I'm not going anywhere."

"You're an important man, Matt. I understand that you have responsibilities. I'll be okay up here alone."

"I'll try my cell phone in the morning. If it doesn't work, I'll drive into town and call my secretary. She'll take care of it."

Through the last traces of daylight she eyed him doubtfully. "You're sure?"

About as sure as he could be in his present state of mind. "Finish up in the kitchen and meet me down at the beach."

"What are you going to do?"

"Gather wood. We're having a bonfire."

Nine

By the time Emily made her way down the dark path to the beach, equipped with the fixings for s'mores, Matt had the fire blazing. When she saw the blanket he'd brought down with him, she stopped dead in her tracks. It wasn't the presence of the blanket that gave her pause, but its placement. He'd spread it in the sand in the exact spot they'd sat that night. No way it wasn't deliberate.

She should have been damned angry about it, but all she could do was picture herself and Matt lying there, bodies intertwined. This time the boundaries of their relationship were drawn. Friendship, with a little hot sex thrown in to spice things up. There were pros and cons, of course. And honestly, she was beginning to believe the pros greatly outweighed the cons. She'd already mostly decided that if he made another move on her, she might not fight it. She might let nature take its course and see what happened.

She walked to the blanket and sat down. Crickets chirped in the woods and she heard the rush of the waves as they slapped against the shore. The fire crackled and hissed and sent plumes of smoke drifting up into the trees. It felt peaceful, serene—until Matt tossed one more log into the fire, the orange glow accentuating the muscle tone in his arms and thighs, and she was flooded with an overload of female hormones. She felt the same giddy nervousness as she had on the last night they'd spent here. Would he kiss her? Would he touch her? Would she have the courage to make the first move if he didn't?

Matt dropped down on the blanket beside her. Close enough to be friendly, and far enough away to be frustrating. "I think that's enough fire to last awhile."

"I brought stuff for s'mores." She opened the bag of marshmallows, loaded the skewers, and handed one to Matt.

"I haven't done this in years," he said, holding his close to the flame.

Emily held her own beside Matt's. She wasn't really in the mood for sweets—not unless she was licking them off his body. What she was really craving was the taste of his mouth, the saltiness of his skin.

Any time now you can try to seduce me, she thought. Instead he stared into the fire, slowly twirling his skewer, and asked, "I noticed that you never answered my question."

"What question was that?"

"I asked if you're in love with Alex."

"I am," she said. "But not in the way you think. The truth is, we see other people."

She could swear she saw relief in his eyes.

"But you can't tell my parents," she added. "Or my brother."

"Why not?"

"To preserve my sanity." At his quizzical look, she added, "My parents are determined to get me married off. I won't sit through one more dinner with some employee of my father's, or the son of a family friend. Having a boyfriend is the only way to get them off my back."

"Why don't you just tell them to stop?"

"Matt, you of all people should know that would never work. They just don't listen."

"Would it hurt to try?"

"*Try?* I've spent my entire life trying." A familiar rush of resentment swelled to the surface. "I've had to fight for my independence. As long as I can remember, they've been making decisions based on what they think is good for me. When I wanted to play T-ball, my mom signed me up for ballet. Instead of letting me play soccer, my parents put me in gymnastics. In kindergarten, my mom decided wearing jeans like Ty wasn't appropriate for a girl and forced me to wear dresses."

"I don't remember ever seeing you wear a dress, so you must have won that battle."

"Yeah, because I started lifting my dress and showing boys my underpants."

Matt laughed. "You didn't."

"Don't you think it's sad that at six years old I had to go to such an extreme? It was like they just couldn't accept me for the person I was supposed to be. They still don't.''

"They just want what's best for you.''

"But who are *they* to decide what's best for me? Suppose I'm not ready to settle down?''

He wondered if he should tell Emily what her family was up to, and immediately decided it would be a bad idea. He didn't want to give her the idea that his feelings for her weren't genuine, that they'd put him up to it. Even though technically they had. And there was no way he could mention any of what she'd just said to her family. He would never betray her trust that way. In other words, he was caught in the middle.

This also meant she wouldn't be quitting her job, which presented him with a entirely new problem— how to find out what Alex was up to. Maybe he should just come right out and tell her his suspicions. Maybe she'd seen something fishy and would put two and two together. If he said nothing, and she found herself in trouble with the law because of it, he would never forgive himself.

"How, um, trustworthy is Alex?''

She mushed a piece of chocolate and a golden brown marshmallow between two crackers. "I would trust him with my life. Why do you ask?''

"It's just that, I've heard things.''

"What things?'' She took a bite, warm chocolate and marshmallow dripping down her chin. Oh, man, did he want to lick it away for her.

"He goes out of the country a lot?''

She sucked chocolate off her fingers. "A couple of times a year. He travels with friends.''

"You get shipments from other countries?''

"Now and then. Most are domestic. Uh, Matt?" She nodded toward the fire, and he realized his marshmallow had gone up in flames.

He shook it off the skewer and it landed with a sizzling splat in the embers.

"Here, take a bite of mine." She held it out for him, chocolate oozing down his chin as he bit off a piece.

"Messy," she said, wiping it off with her thumb and holding it up to his mouth. She wanted him to...*oh, man.* He opened his mouth and she slid her thumb over his tongue. He couldn't speak. He couldn't even breathe.

What had they been talking about?

"Why are you suddenly so interested in Alex?" she asked, reminding him. Only he didn't want to talk about her boyfriend now. He wanted to lick melted chocolate off her entire body.

Focus, Conway. This is important. "Do you know what he does when he leaves the country?"

"I have a pretty good idea."

"Are you sure?"

"Matt, why don't you tell me what you're insinuating?"

"Word is circulating that he might be involved in something...shady."

"Shady?"

"Drugs, Em."

Instead of looking concerned, Emily snorted out a laugh. "*Drugs?* You're kidding, right?"

"You could be putting yourself in trouble just working for him."

"I'm not in danger of anything."

"How can you be sure?"

She tossed what was left of her s'more into the fire. "I see every shipment that goes in or out of that nursery. I track every penny. There's no way he could be running drugs through without me knowing about it. I mean, the guy can't even remember to pay the electric bill on time. Who could possibly have had a harebrained idea like—no wait. Don't tell me. *Ty* told you."

His expression must have said it all.

She shook her head. "He's such an idiot."

"He's genuinely worried about you, Em."

"No, he doesn't like Alex, and he doesn't want anyone else to like him either." She started gathering the food. "It's late. If we're going to get up early to fish we should get to bed."

"Em—"

"I'm angry, Conway. Not at you. Just ticked off in general and I wouldn't be very good company. I'll see you in the morning."

He watched as she disappeared through the woods.

He'd blown it. A minute ago she'd been taking the initiative, letting him suck chocolate off her fingers. She would have been his, if he'd just kept quiet.

She was wrong about Ty. He wasn't an idiot.

Matt was.

Emily lay in bed staring at the wood beams above her, unable to sleep, so angry she could spit nails. The small fan on the dresser across the room just circulated the hot, muggy air. Dressed in only panties and a tank top, her skin was slick with sweat, making the sheets stick to her like fly paper. She grabbed her watch off the night table and checked the time. One-ten in the morning.

It was one thing for Ty to tell people he didn't care for Alex. She'd gotten used to that. But to spread rumors that he was peddling *drugs?* That was over the top even for Ty. And as badly as Emily wanted to throttle him, if she let on that Matt told her, it could drive a wedge between Ty and Matt. She just had to be angry until she wasn't angry anymore.

Too hot and sticky even to consider sleep, she rolled out of bed and tugged on a pair of shorts. Maybe it would be cooler by the water. She shoved her feet into her flip-flops and tiptoed into the hall, stopping outside Matt's room.

The door was open and she could see the outline of his body sprawled across the twin-size mattress. He was so large and the mattress so small it was almost comical. It had to be a major step down from the luxury he was accustomed to. She had offered her parents' room, but he had said he wouldn't feel right sleeping there.

So here he was cramped into a bed he'd dwarfed even in high school. She couldn't hear his breathing over the hum of the fan, but his chest rose and fell in a steady rhythm. His *bare* chest, she noticed with a giddy, light-headed feeling. He was covered to the waist with a sheet and she had to wonder what, if anything, he wore underneath. In high school he'd worn boxers to bed. At least, when he'd spent the night at their house he had. She would sometimes walk by Ty's room in the morning and get a glimpse of Matt on the spare bed, sprawled out much as he was now, wearing boxers.

Back then, considering her pathetic lack of experience with the opposite sex, she'd lived for moments like that. She'd felt naughty for spying on him, but it had thrilled her no end to see him that way. So vulnerable. So peaceful. Once she'd peeked in and had gotten more than she'd bargained for when she'd realized his boxers were fitting tighter than usual. A *lot* tighter.

She'd gone beet red with embarrassment and something else, a breathless feeling that had drained all the energy from her muscles and made them quiver. She hadn't been able to pull herself away. She wanted to know what he was hiding under his shorts. Only when she heard her mother coming up the stairs had she dashed down the hall and closed herself into the bathroom.

The feeling she hadn't recognized back then had become more than clear that night on the beach. It had been pure lust. The same thing she was feeling now.

Matt sighed in his sleep and rolled away from her, dragging the sheet with him. From the looks of it, he didn't wear boxers to bed anymore. Now, he didn't wear *anything*.

Her estrogen production instantly went hyperactive.

She gazed at the smooth contour of his bare muscular behind, wishing she could crawl into bed with him. Things had been moving along so well by the fire. When she'd slipped her thumb in his mouth she'd thought for sure his eyes would bulge right out of his head, and she'd nearly melted into a puddle when she'd run her thumb across his tongue. Licking what was left off his chin would have been her next move, had he not dropped the bomb.

Alex running drugs. Ridiculous.

No, not just ridiculous—laughable.

She backed away from Matt's room and headed to the kitchen. She grabbed a beer from the fridge and a beach blanket from the porch on her way out and headed down to the water, feeling her way through the thick underbrush alongside the path. The stifling heat was only slightly less oppressive outside, and the idea of a midnight swim held even greater appeal. On the beach, the fire had just about burned itself out, so she grabbed a few logs and tossed them on the embers. Instantly the parched wood ignited and flames licked up to encompass them.

Emily spread the blanket out, kicked off her shoes and walked down to the water sipping her beer. Across the lake fires dotted the beach and if she strained hard enough she could hear the faintest sound of music and laughter. That should have been her and Matt. Sitting up half the night, laughing and talking about old times. Then reliving them in vivid detail.

Emotion burned the back of her throat and left a bitter taste in her mouth. Tomorrow night, she promised herself. She'd make it up to him. To herself.

Away from the fire, it was so dark she had to keep a hand stretched out in front of her to feel her way to the dock. She stepped into the cool water, instantly feeling soothed. Maybe a swim would ease the restlessness in her muscles, in her soul.

She set her beer down and slipped her clothes off, leaving them on the dock. It's not as if anyone was going to happen by this time of night, and even if they did it was too dark to see anything. She'd thought the same thing this afternoon on the beach just before Matt had happened by. But he was sound asleep now.

She walked several feet out, then dove in, the cool water working her body loose. She swam out several yards, until her muscles began to burn from the exertion, then rolled over and floated on her back for a while. Her body lifted and swelled with the gentle waves, and above her the sky was a showcase of twinkling lights. She closed her eyes and sighed, letting herself sink down until the water covered her head. She surfaced, disoriented in the dark, then spotted the fire and headed in that direction until the shadowy outline of the dock became clear. She followed it up until she was waist-high, feeling her way, looking for the beer she'd set there. Her hand instead collided with a muscular, hairy leg.

She shrieked and yanked her arm away and heard a rumble of laughter from Matt.

"Are you trying to give me a heart attack!" she admonished.

"Didn't anyone ever teach you not to drink and swim?"

As his shadowy form became clear, she saw him raise something to his lips. Probably her beer. "What are you doing out here?"

"Watching you skinny-dip, I think. These *are* your clothes I'm holding, aren't they?"

Her hands automatically flew up to cover her breasts. "I thought you were sleeping."

"I was faking it." She made a sound of indignation and he laughed again. "You didn't seem to mind so much when you were looking at my butt."

"You did that on purpose?" Embarrassment set her face on fire.

"You didn't have to wait until I was sleeping. All you had to do was ask and I would have shown it to you."

Faint light penetrated the darkness and she could almost make out the smirk she heard so clearly in his voice. On the beach the bonfire crackled and hissed, spitting flames high into the air. She didn't think she'd built it that large, then realized Matt must have added wood.

He set her beer down on the dock and stood, looming high above her as he shoved his shorts down his legs and kicked them away. She could see enough to know that he was as magnificently built as he had been in high school. She stood enraptured, unable to make herself look away as he slipped almost soundlessly down in the water beside her.

"I was getting lonely in bed all by myself," he said. She heard husky desire in his voice and he circled her in the water, like a shark stalking its intended victim.

Her heart hammered in her chest and she closed her eyes, waited to feel his hands on her skin. She shivered in anticipation, but he didn't touch her. Finally she turned to him and realized he was gone. He resurfaced several yards away from her, shaking water from his hair.

"Aren't you going to swim?" he asked, treading water.

Actually I was thinking more along the lines of screaming sex, thank you.

It was time she took the initiative, even if she did have zero experience seducing men. And suppose he'd changed his mind and didn't want her anymore? If she came on to him, and he rejected her, she wasn't sure she could take that. It had taken her years to work up the courage to tell him her feelings the first time. Although, since he'd been back, he'd been pretty relentless in his pursuit. And she'd been pretty relentless in her refusal.

She pushed herself backward into the water, sinking below the surface, then rising up to float on her back.

Matt watched her. Backlit by the fire blazing on the beach, the silhouette of her breasts bobbed temptingly in and out of the water. In and out. He couldn't wait to get a good look at them, to take that nipple ring between his teeth. It had nearly become an obsession.

In his life, he didn't think he'd ever been so mystified by the idea of touching a woman. Of course, in his life, he'd never met another woman quite like Emily. When he'd heard her standing in the hallway, he'd hoped she would climb into his bed, not that they both would have fitted in it. He liked the idea of making love to her on the beach again even more. Their eleven-year reunion. They could make it a tradition. Although he wasn't sure he wanted to wait another eleven years to be with her again. Maybe this should be an annual event. Monthly would work, too. Daily and he would be in heaven.

Maybe after the restaurant was built. Maybe then he could slow down, think seriously about exploring a committed relationship with a woman. With Emily. If she wanted that from him.

He swam closer to her, but stayed far enough away that he wouldn't be tempted to touch, enjoying this heightened anticipation. Each time she drifted toward him, he drifted away.

Finally, she rose in the water, naked from the waist up, her skin glistening, her pert breasts begging to be caressed. Oh, man. Not touching her was going to be hell.

But something wasn't right, something in her body language told him she wasn't having nearly as much fun with this as he was. Then she reached up to shield her breasts and he knew he was losing her.

"I think I'll go back to bed now," she said, turning away from him and wading toward the beach.

"Em, wait." He followed, grabbing her arm to stop her. "Why are you leaving?"

"You obviously don't want me out here." Her voice quivered and he realized she was genuinely upset. "Every time I come near you, you move away."

"I'm sorry, Em." He pulled her to him. She was a bundle of warmth and softness against him. And that was what he'd forgotten. Emily had a soft, vulnerable side. Unlike the women he normally came into contact with, the barracudas. The ones who didn't hesitate to let a man know exactly what they wanted, and what they were willing to give in return.

What had made him think Emily would be one of those women?

He felt like a jerk because he'd never stopped to look at it from Emily's point of view. He'd come back after ignoring her for more than a decade, chased her for days, and when she finally made a move toward him, he moved away. What the hell had he been thinking?

"You're confusing me," she said softly. "Do you want me or not?"

"Yes, I do." He held her snugly against him. "I

was acting like an idiot. I'm sorry. I thought it might be fun if I could get you to chase me for a while. I guess my ego needed stroking.''

''You could have any woman in the world, Matt. Why does it matter if I chase you?''

He drew back and cupped her face in his hands. ''Because of all the women in the world, the only one I want is you.''

Ten

He'd said the words out loud—words he'd denied for more years than he cared to admit—and the world hadn't come crashing down around him. It actually felt good to finally have it out in the open, as if he'd been released somehow.

Emily only smiled, smoothing a hand across his cheek. He couldn't tell if she believed him, or thought he was just humoring her. But then it didn't matter, because she looped her arms around his neck, pulled his face to hers and kissed him.

It started with a bang, hot and deep and full of passion, and it only got hotter. Once she got into her comfort zone, she was an explosion waiting to happen. He was so blown away, for a second he only stood there, barely able to keep up as she ravished him. It was as if she was starving and only the taste of his mouth could satisfy her. The buzz of mosquitoes around his head, the cool water lapping against his waist, all faded into the background. There was only Emily. Her lithe body forming just right against him, her breasts a soft contrast to the hard planes of his chest.

He wrapped his arms around her, smoothing his hands across her shoulders, down her back. Every inch of her skin felt exquisitely soft. Naturally soft. Somehow he couldn't imagine Emily seeking the aid of expensive creams or spa treatments. Everything about her was natural and pure. Which was more than he could say about the thoughts running through his head. They were anything but pure.

He cupped her behind, and she moaned into his mouth, arching against him. "Cottage or beach?" he asked, leaving the decision up to her, though he had a definite preference.

She didn't disappoint him. She smiled up at him and said, "Definitely the beach."

He lifted her up out of the water and she locked her legs around his waist, her arms around his neck. Still, as he started toward the beach she began sliding out of his grip. "It's hard to impress you with my strength and charm when you're this slippery. Hang on tight or I may drop you."

The arms around his neck tightened and she whispered, "Don't worry, I'm already impressed."

When they reached the blanket he dropped to his knees and set her down. They stretched out together, and though he felt he couldn't wait another second to make love to her, he could do nothing but stare. They lay side by side for the longest time simply looking at each other. It had been so long since he'd seen her this way he'd almost forgotten how damned perfect she was, and maybe in his youth he hadn't completely grasped what she'd so eagerly offered him. No supermodel or actress he'd known could hold a candle to her beauty. It shone from both inside and out. What she'd given him that night was a gift. One that he hadn't fully appreciated until now, now that he'd realized just how empty his life had been without her in it.

He hadn't had time for her then. Suppose now he could *make* time. What would she say if he asked her to come back to California with him? The possibility buzzed in his head, making his heart race. Was he ready to make that kind of commitment?

The only thing he knew for sure, was that nothing had ever felt as right as holding Emily in his arms. Not back then, and certainly not now.

Firelight danced across her moist skin. He gazed at her lush mouth as it drew up into a semi-shy smile. There was nothing about her that didn't turn him on. Her body was long and lean yet so soft and feminine. She'd matured, filled out just the right amount in all the right places. His eyes were drawn to the gold ring in her left nipple. It glinted in the firelight, shimmering against her tawny skin.

"Damn, that's pretty." He reached up to skim his finger around it, then closed his eyes and sighed. "My life is complete."

Emily laughed lightly. "You're sure easy to please."

"You have no idea how much I've wanted to see this. And do this..." Holding her gaze, he lowered his head and gently took the ring in his teeth.

Emily's lips parted and her eyelids grew heavy.

He tugged just a little bit and she gasped lightly. "Sensitive, huh?"

"Hmm," she said, a dreamy look on her face.

"I don't suppose you would consider getting the other one done." He tugged again, a bit harder, and the dreamy look became one of pure ecstasy.

"I might."

And if she did, would he be around to enjoy it? Or would he wake in the morning and realize he wasn't ready to commit his life to anyone yet? Could he be happy with Emily, all the while fighting the feeling that something was still missing? Would it be fair to her?

She brushed a finger across his nipple and he shivered. "Maybe you could get yours done, too."

If it would make her happy, he might consider it. There wasn't much she could ask of him right now that he wouldn't do.

Lowering his head, he took the ring and the entire blush peak of her nipple into his mouth, tasting the tang of metal and Emily's own unique flavor. Emily moaned, tunneling her fingers through his hair.

So the other nipple wouldn't feel left out, he leaned over and flicked that one lightly with his tongue. After only a minute the ring called to him like a magnet and he couldn't stay away.

He felt Emily's hands trail downward. Over his chest, across his stomach. His pulse surged and liquid desire saturated his blood. When her hand wrapped around him, it felt so damned wonderful he could have passed out.

She pushed him onto his back and rose up on her elbow as she stroked him. His eyes were glued to the movements of her hand. She lowered her head and swiped the sensitive tip with her tongue and his body coiled with pleasure.

Her eyes never leaving his face, she took him deep into her mouth. If it were anyone but Emily the sight wouldn't have been half as erotic. Her total lack of inhibitions still blew his mind. That first night, she'd taken whatever he was willing to give, and didn't hesitate to give back in return. He could see that hadn't changed.

When it would have been so easy to lie back and enjoy it, he rose up on his elbows, knowing instinctively she needed eye contact. It had been like that before. She never took her eyes off his face, as if she thought that when she looked away he might cease to exist. It had been so intimate, so deeply personal. He'd felt a connection with her he'd yet to experience with another woman.

The pleasure in his groin began to build, radiating out until he felt his control slipping. With his eyes on her every move, it was impossible not to lose it. She was just so…hot, yet there was an innocence to her actions that mystified him. He groaned and let his head fall back. "Em, stop. I'm too close."

"I can keep going," Emily said. He had no idea how long she'd wanted to do that again. To see that look of rapture, of total submission. He had no idea how arousing she found it. "I will if you want me to."

Eyes closed, chest heaving, Matt shook his head.

"It didn't feel good?"

He looked up at her, his eyes so dark with desire they looked jet-black. "It felt *too* good. Ladies first."

"You're sure?" she asked, licking her way across his belly.

He tangled his fingers in her hair and ground out between his teeth, ''You're making it really difficult for me to do the right thing.''

''Sexist garbage,'' she said, lowering her head to take him into her mouth again. And the next thing she knew, he'd flipped her over and pinned her to the blanket. Damn, he was quick. ''No fair.''

''Sue me,'' he said, a grin on his face. He perused her body in a way that made her skin feel too hot and tight. He took her nipple ring between his teeth again, tugging lightly, and her stomach almost turned itself inside out the pleasure was so deep. He switched to the other side, scraped the nipple lightly with his teeth, then closed his mouth over the entire peak and sucked so deeply she cried out.

He backed off to admire his work. The firm tip glistened with moisture and was tinted deep red from the intense suction. ''Perfect.''

''Not big enough,'' she said, so breathless she barely had enough air to get the words out.

''Emily, your breasts are perfect.'' He kissed each one gently. ''Everything about you is perfect.''

If he was lying, she didn't even care. She just wanted him to keep touching her.

He kissed his way down to the lowermost edge of her rib cage, stopping to caress, to taste. Then lower, down the center of her belly, around her navel. For every inch he sank, her pulse quickened. Watching her, he slipped between her thighs, pressing them apart. Exactly the way he had that first night. And she was filled with the same restless anticipation. She'd heard girls in school giggle and whisper about oral sex. It sounded so private. So forbidden. So...*wonderful*. But she didn't think people really did it. Adults maybe, with years and years of experience. But not teenagers. Then Matt had slipped down between her legs and she'd known what was coming next, and she'd *wanted* it.

There hadn't been anything she wasn't willing to try. Matt had given her her first orgasm that way. And she hadn't hesitated to return the gesture, finding that the girls at school had been dead wrong. There had been nothing gross about it. The look on Matt's face alone, the blind pleasure, knowing *she* was making him feel that way, had made it worthwhile. She'd had so many firsts that night, each more wondrous than the last.

"You're thinking about that night," Matt said.

"Yeah," she murmured. He always seemed to know just what was going on in her head. Sometimes so keenly it scared her.

"Are you remembering the way I touched you?" Matt's rough chin grazed her sensitive inner thigh and she shuddered.

"Uh-huh."

"Like when I did this?" He lowered his head, touching her lightly with his tongue.

Her body tensed and rocked upward.

"Easy." Flattening his hand against her stomach, he held her down. "Relax."

Relax? Was he kidding? She was on *fire* here.

He did it again, stroking with his tongue. So frustratingly light. She had to fight to keep her body still, not to arch up against his mouth. He stopped altogether to kiss her inner thigh. Then the other thigh. Then he was suddenly fascinated with touching the back of her knee. Then her ankle!

He was moving in the wrong direction. Not that it

wasn't all sheer ecstasy, but a woman could only take so much.

She made an impatient noise to move things along.

He lifted his head and looked at her. "You in a hurry, or something?"

"I don't remember it taking this long last time."

"That's usually the case when you're a teenager," he said, then went back to work on her other ankle. By the time he worked his way to her thigh she was sure the anticipation would do her in.

Finally he was pressing her legs even farther apart, and he was…oh! Biting. So softly it was barely more than a tease. She dug her fingers into his damp hair where it curled at his nape, so he couldn't get away again. He nibbled here, tasted there…completely missing his target. Maybe he'd forgotten how, or needed a refresher course in anatomy.

She cleared her throat.

"Don't rush me," he mumbled.

While she was sure she would go out of her mind, he concentrated on that tender, aching, tangle of nerves—

Emily groaned and pressed up hard but Matt held her firmly in place. Her body tied itself into a million aching little knots and her vision went blurry. Pleasure built inside her slowly, like waves lapping gently against the sand, and just before she reached a crest, before release set her free, Matt sat up.

Still teetering on the edge of complete bliss, her mouth refused to form words. She could only moan her displeasure at his abrupt departure.

"Look at me, Em," he said.

She opened her eyes and found Matt braced over her, lowering himself between her thighs. He was going to make love to her again. She almost couldn't believe it was really happening. For only the briefest of moments did she entertain the notion that it might hurt, then he was inside her. He filled her so completely, she gasped at the sudden invasion.

"Oh, Em," he groaned, and she knew he'd felt it, too. One look at his face and she was lost again. Pleasure caused her muscles to clench and flex around him. Every thrust propelled her higher, each level more excruciatingly wonderful than the next, until the pleasure finally peaked and exploded in a brilliant spectrum of color.

She clung to him, awash with sensation as Matt drove hard inside her and she felt him reach his own shuddering release. He stilled and settled against her and for a minute they both lay there, quietly catching their breath, arms and legs intertwined. In her life she'd never been closer to another person. Not physically, not spiritually.

It was official, Matt had completely ruined her for other men.

He lifted his head from where it had been resting on her shoulder. "You okay?"

She looked up at him with eyelids she couldn't quite keep open all the way. "You have to ask?"

"Just making sure." He kissed the tip of her nose, her jaw, the corner of her mouth. "If I didn't know any better, I would think…" He shook his head. "Never mind."

"No, tell me," she said. "You would think what?"

"You were just so…" He paused, as if he couldn't identify the word he sought.

"So…?"

"*Tight.* It's almost like you haven't done this since…" He shook his head again, a rueful smile coaxing out his dimple. "Just wishful thinking on my part, I guess."

Emily bit her lip and looked away. So he had been able to tell. Not that it was something she was trying to hide. But it was a little embarrassing.

Matt frowned. "You're not saying anything. You always have some sort of sassy comeback. What's the deal?" He lifted her chin with his index finger, forcing her to look him in the eye. "Em?"

The truth must have been plastered all over her face. It would explain the look of disbelief plastered all over Matt's.

"Don't you dare think for a minute that I was saving myself for you, or something pathetic like that," she said firmly.

"You mean, you really haven't been with anyone else?"

"What happened between us was just so…special. Everyone says the first time is awful. For me it was perfect. It was everything I'd hoped it would be. I guess I didn't want to ruin that."

"For me, it was never the same as…" His brow furrowed deeply.

"The same as what?"

He shrugged. "I don't know."

The same as being with me? she wanted to ask. It was what she desperately wanted to hear.

A cool breeze kicked off the water and Emily shivered. She gathered herself closer to Matt, sinking into his warmth. Then she had a sudden revelation, and the shiver turned into a shudder of fear. "Tell me we did use birth control."

Matt grinned. "Yeah, we did. I brought a condom with me when I came out and left it under the corner of the blanket."

Her entire being sighed with relief. "I'm glad one of us was thinking ahead."

Matt lifted his head, eyes scanning the tree line.

"What's wrong?"

"I'm hoping no one is out there with night-vision goggles."

"Or a telephoto lens?"

His eyes widened. "Jeez, I never even thought about that. I didn't tell anyone where I was going. I doubt the tabloids would ever think to look for me here."

Apprehension slid down her spine. "I was only kidding. The tabloids actually follow you?"

"Occasionally. It was particularly obnoxious after the *People* article. But my secretary knows not to give out personal information. Like where I'm staying."

"Maybe to be on the safe side we should go back to the cottage. I don't even like looking at my bare behind in the mirror. The last place I want to see it is on the cover of a magazine."

"What about our clothes?"

She looked over in the direction of the dock. It was too dark to find much of anything out there. "We'll get them tomorrow."

"You want to walk through the woods *naked?*"

"What's wrong?" she teased. "Are you afraid of the dark?"

"Actually, I'm afraid of certain protruding parts of my anatomy getting caught on a low-hanging tree branch."

She winced. "Yeah, that would be bad. How about if we wrap up in the blanket?"

"That'll work."

Emily shook out the blanket while Matt tossed sand on the fire to douse it. Since walking through the woods barefoot was a health hazard, they put their sandals on, wrapped themselves in the blanket, and stumbled back to the cottage, laughing at how ridiculous they would look to anyone who might see them that way.

When they reached the cottage it was nearly 3:00 a.m. As soon as they were inside he wrapped his arms around her waist from behind and dropped kisses across her shoulder.

"We're supposed to be up in an hour to fish," Emily reminded him.

"I choose making love all night and sleeping till noon over fishing any day. In fact, I wouldn't be opposed to spending the entire weekend in bed. How about you?"

She slipped her arms over his, lacing their fingers together. Two weeks ago, if someone had told her she would be standing naked in her parents' cottage with Matt, she would have said there wasn't a chance in hell. Yet here they were, Matt leading her to her bedroom. Matt lying down next to her in her bed. Matt making love to her until hints of dawn crept in through the open window. Until they lay sated and limp, yet too awake to sleep.

Unbelievable.

"What are you thinking about?" Matt asked.

"How different my life was a week ago." She gazed up at him through the hazy light, idly traced the line of his stubbled jaw with her index finger. ''How unexpected this has been.''

''Unexpected good, or unexpected bad?''

''Unexpected good, as in, I'll be really sorry to see it end.''

''Maybe it doesn't have to.''

''We'll always be friends, but we both know it can't be more than that.''

''Maybe it could.''

She dashed the tiny kernel of hope that began to grow inside her. ''How many serious relationships have you been in since you left Michigan?''

A frown slashed across his face. ''None.''

''Have you *ever* had a serious relationship?''

''That doesn't mean I'm incapable. California is a nice place to live. You would like it.'' There was so much hope in his voice, she ached inside.

''What about work? You said before that you had no time for a relationship.''

''I can make time.''

''How much time, and for how long? Are you talking a month? A year? A lifetime? You're still going to feel like something is missing, and you're going to want to find it. You'll start working crazy hours again. Eventually I'll get tired of being alone all the time, and you'll get tired of me complaining, until our relationship is nothing but a burden.''

He looked hurt by what she knew to be reality. Even if he didn't want to admit it. ''It doesn't have to be that way.''

''I have dreams, too, Matt. Things I want to do with my life. You're asking me to sacrifice it all. To move to a strange place where I know no one, where I have no family.''

"Emily, I can take care of you. I can give you anything you want."

"Your time, Matt. Can you give me that?"

He didn't answer. As she'd expected, it was more than he was willing to give.

She lay beside him, resting her cheek against his chest, listening to the steady thrum of his heart. "You're asking me to sacrifice so much, yet you're willing to give practically nothing in return. How long do you think we'll last that way?"

He tightened his arms around her. "You make it sound hopeless."

"It is what it is. We're together now. Let's just enjoy each other's company while you're here and not worry about what we'll be doing a month from now. And who knows, by then, we could be tired of each other."

"You can be a real pain in the behind," he said, humor in his voice. "And incredibly stubborn."

"And you can be sexist and overbearing." And perfect in a million other tiny ways. And she would never get tired of him. But some things simply weren't meant to be.

She lay in his arms drifting off to sleep, realizing she was living out the second half of her fantasy—exactly what she had wished would have happened that night eleven years ago. To fall asleep in Matt's arms. There were no parents to walk in on them, no schedules to follow. No businesses to worry about. For the entire weekend, it was just her and Matt.

Eleven

"**E**mily! Matt! Where are you?"

Emily bolted up in bed, jolted awake by a nightmare. She looked dazedly around until the room came into focus, grateful to find it empty. She'd dreamed her mother called to her, that she was there at the cottage. If her parents saw her and Matt this way, naked, rumpled and sleeping in her bed, they would freak. Or even worse, they would think this meant something. They would think she and Matt were in love. Heaven knows they would like nothing more than to have Matt for a son-in-law, and half a dozen mini-Matt grandchildren running around.

If her parents had even a hint that something was brewing between Emily and Matt, they would relentlessly hound them to get married. That would *really* be a nightmare, considering their conversation last night.

Beside her, Matt mumbled in his sleep and rolled onto his side. The initial horror of her dream behind her, she yawned and lay back down, curling up behind him.

"Emily! Matt! Are you here?"

At the sound of her mother's voice, she shot up in bed again, clutching the sheets to cover herself. It wasn't a dream. Her mother was really here.

She muttered a curse and jumped out of bed, taking the sheet with her. She slammed the bedroom door shut and flattened her body against it.

This could not possibly be happening.

Matt sat up in bed, bleary-eyed, rumpled and unbelievably sexy. "What happened? Where did the covers go?"

"Shh," she hissed. "Don't say anything."

There was a loud rap on the door, then her mother's worried voice. "Emily, are you okay?"

"Fine, Mom, I'm just not dressed yet."

"What happened to Matt? His vehicle is here but we can't find him."

She cringed and said nonchalantly, "He's probably out jogging or something. Give me a minute to get dressed and I'll help you find him."

"We'll wait in the living room," her mother called, then Emily heard her receding footsteps.

"I guess this rules out morning sex," Matt mumbled from behind her.

She turned to him. He was sitting up in bed, his hair disheveled, his eyes cloudy from sleep. And sexy. Lord, did he look sexy. This was so unfair. She wanted her morning sex. "We have to get rid of them."

He raked a hand through his rumpled hair and yawned. "Okay."

"You'll have to jump out the window," she said.

"*Naked?* All my clothes are in the next room."

"Wear this." She tossed the sheet at him and rummaged through her bag for a pair of shorts and a top. She tugged her shorts on and wrestled the shirt over her head.

Matt cursed under his breath and climbed out of bed, wrapping the sheet around his waist. What a way to end one of the hottest nights of his life. "I am not jumping out a window."

"We can't let them see you."

Didn't he know it. He could just imagine it now. Yes, Mr. and Mrs. Douglas, I did violate your trust, and your daughter, who I don't happen to be in love with. Oh, and by the way, I have this favor to ask...

Talk about slitting your own throat.

"Take them outside and pretend you're looking for me," he said. "Tell them you think I'm down at the beach. While you're gone, I'll get dressed, head through the woods on the other side and circle around to the beach."

"I'm so sorry about this," she said, her eyes apologetic. "I didn't want our night to end this way."

Amen to that. "Just go distract them."

Emily paused by the door, then turned and pressed a quick kiss to his lips. "I'll make it up to you when they leave."

With a smile that promised she would live up to that statement, she slipped out the door. And all Matt could think about was getting rid of her parents. But not before he talked to them about the property. That was too important to put off. He had the entire weekend to lose himself in the wonders of Emily's body.

He pressed his ear to the door and listened, heard the anxious tone in her mother's voice and the disappointed edge to her father's, but he couldn't hear what was being said. A minute later he heard the screen door slam shut and figured the coast was clear. He slipped out of Emily's bedroom and into his own. He threw on some clothes, combed his fingers through his hair, and headed for the door. As he was reaching for the handle he heard voices, then Emily pulled the door open and stepped inside, followed by her parents.

He stood there, mouth hanging open, too surprised to speak.

"See, I told you I heard the door," Emily said to her mother, then turned to Matt. "We've been looking for you. How was your walk?"

"Great," he said, following her lead. "It was good."

"There you are, Matt," Mrs. Douglas said, looking distressed. "We were so worried about you. We got your message and you said it was urgent. We tried to call but you never returned our messages and your office said they couldn't reach you either. Then we couldn't get a hold of Emily. We thought something was wrong."

"Ty said you were coming here," Mr. Douglas said, an identical look of concern on his face. "We thought something had happened to one of you."

"And of course Emily refuses to carry a cellular phone," Emily's mother said, shooting her daughter a stern look, as if Emily not owning a phone was some sort of slight against her mother.

"I'm sorry to have alarmed you and made you drive all this way," Matt said. "The urgent issue I had with you was business-related."

"Oh, I'm so glad." Mrs. Douglas fanned herself dramatically, as if she might pass out with relief.

"What kind of business?" Mr. Douglas asked.

Emily took her parents by the arm and ushered them toward the door. "You've had such a long drive and it's so hot in the cottage. Why don't you two sit on the porch while Matt and I get some cool drinks together, then you can talk business."

When they were settled outside, Emily hooked an arm through Matt's and pulled him toward the kitchen. Her skin was damp and sweat beaded her brow. She said in a hushed tone, "Phew, that was close."

"Why did you bring them back? I barely had time to get dressed."

She opened the fridge and pulled out a pitcher of lemonade. She pressed it to her forehead, closed her eyes, and sighed. "We got halfway through the woods when I realized we'd left all our clothes on the dock. And probably a condom wrapper in the sand. I almost had a coronary."

Matt took four glasses down from the cupboard. He'd never even considered the mess they'd left. Thank goodness for Emily's quick thinking. "Sorry I caused all this trouble. When I called your parents I never imagined they would take my message so out of context."

"That's my mother, the drama queen. To hear her talk when we were walking down to the beach, you would have thought she was disappointed we were both intact and breathing." Emily dropped ice into the glasses and poured the lemonade, curious about the nature of this business Matt needed to discuss, and even more curious to know why he hadn't mentioned it to her. And maybe just a little hurt. "You never said anything to me about business with my parents."

He regarded her with a raised brow. "Would you have wanted me to talk about business this weekend?"

Good point. "You're right. It probably would have annoyed me." She picked up two glasses, and Matt took the remaining two. "Ready?"

"The sooner we get this over with, the sooner we'll be alone," Matt said, and the hungry look in his eyes made her heart lurch with anticipation.

They walked out to the porch and distributed the drinks, then took seats next to her parents.

"So, what kind of business do you need to discuss?" her father said, in his typical, no-nonsense way.

In that instant, Matt's demeanor changed. It was subtle, but unmistakable. He sat a little taller, his back straighter, and his expression was serious. This was the all-business Matt she'd wondered about. The one she'd had only a glimpse of at the restaurant the other day.

"I don't know if you've heard," Matt said. "Construction on the restaurant has been stopped."

Emily's mother let out a gasp. "But why?"

"There are certain people in town who don't want me building this restaurant. People in positions of power who have a grudge against me. They don't like that I've come back to town and they've fought the restaurant every step of the way. And this time they might have won.''

Emily could see the passion in his eyes, and the hurt as he explained his dilemma with the square footage. Somehow it didn't surprise her. There were a lot of people who resented Matt's accomplishments.

She was ashamed to admit, she'd been one of those people.

''So you see,'' he concluded. ''If I have to tear the restaurant down and rebuild, we would go way over budget and I could lose backing from my investors. They're already shaky.''

''We could invest in the restaurant,'' Emily's father said, but Matt shook his head.

''I could never ask you to do that. It would be too risky.''

''There has to be some way we can help you,'' Emily's mother said.

The business facade slipped and Emily could see a hint of desperation in Matt's eyes, and she suddenly understood how important this was to him. He needed to do this for the same reason she needed to build her shop.

''There's a simple way to solve this. You could sell me the vacant lot next to the restaurant.''

Emily's parents exchanged looks, and she cringed inwardly. Matt was asking for something her parents just couldn't do. They had promised that property to her. And if it weren't the absolute perfect location for a flower shop, she might have sacrificed the property and built elsewhere. But Chapel already had two other flower shops, both on the opposite end of town.

This was the best spot for her. As a businessman, Matt would understand that.

Her mother leaned forward and patted Matt's knee. Here it comes, Emily thought. The big disappointment.

Her mother gave Matt a thousand-watt smile. "Of course we'll sell you the property."

For a full minute, Emily was too dumbfounded to form words. They must have forgotten they were saving the property for her. That was the only explanation. They wouldn't sell it out from under her. Not when she'd worked so hard for so long.

"We'll settle on a price and I'll have my attorney draw up the contracts," Matt was saying, to which her father readily agreed.

She had to put an end to this before it went too far. She cleared her throat and said, "Excuse me."

All eyes were suddenly on her.

"You can't sell the property to Matt. You promised to sell it to me. Remember?"

There was a moment of dead silence. A sick feeling of dread filled Emily's heart. They wouldn't. They wouldn't dare pick Matt over her. Their own daughter.

Her parents exchanged a look, then her mother turned to her and sighed. "Emily, honey, be reasonable. Where are you going to get the money for that property?"

"I've earned it. I've almost got it all. I just need another six months."

"Then how do you plan to pay for the building?"

"A business loan."

"Honey," her father reasoned in the same voice he would use with a temperamental child. "You have no collateral. No bank in their right mind would loan you money.''

A slap in the face couldn't have hurt any more. ''The property *is* the collateral. That's why I have to buy it outright.''

''Emily,'' her mother said in her ''be reasonable'' voice. ''Chapel doesn't need another flower shop. I think we've entertained this silly little idea of yours for long enough. Matt is a *real* businessman. He *needs* the property.''

''You promised,'' Emily said, her voice quivering. ''You said you would sell the property to me.''

''Soon you'll be married and having children. You won't have time to work. Then what will happen to your little shop?''

''Your mother is right, sweetheart. It's just not reasonable. You know nothing about the intricacies of running a business.''

She was almost too stunned to reply. ''I have a business degree. I've been running the nursery for three years now.''

''And isn't the nursery in danger of going bankrupt?'' her mother snapped.

With the accusation, Emily's heart cracked in two. What she should have realized long ago was now painfully clear. Her parents had no faith in her—no respect for her dreams whatsoever. They had never intended to sell her the property. They were only humoring her.

Nothing had changed. It had never been about what she wanted. Her entire life, all they had ever done was try to change her, to mold her into the kind of daughter *they* dreamed of having. And now they saw her as nothing more than a baby machine, put on this earth to give them grandchildren.

She felt completely and utterly defeated.

Tears burned behind her eyes. With trembling hands she set her lemonade down, stood on wobbly legs and walked into the cottage.

"Emily, wait," Matt called.

She continued on to her bedroom and began shoving her clothes into her duffel bag.

Matt appeared in her doorway. "Emily, I had no idea you wanted that property. You never said anything about a flower shop."

"You're right, I didn't."

"I need that property, Em. If I have to tear down the restaurant and rebuild somewhere different, I'll lose my investors. If I put up all of my own money, and it fails…I can't take that chance."

It all boiled down to money, and him not having enough of it. She zipped her bag shut and slung it over her shoulder. "Then you should be very happy. You got exactly what you wanted."

"There are other lots available."

"That's really not the point, is it?"

"I'll match whatever money you have saved. I'll pay the difference. You can have any property you want. I'll even have my attorneys handle the deal."

Even Matt didn't care about what she wanted. It was all about building his restaurant. All about money. The hollow ache in her chest grew larger, until she could barely breathe. "I'm going home."

She tried to walk past him but he stepped in the way. "Emily, you have to understand what this means to me."

It was always about what he wanted. About what everyone else wanted. It was never about her.

She looked down at the hand on her arm, then up to Matt's face. "I do understand, Conway. Some things never change."

"This is all my fault." Emily buried her face against Alex's work shirt. Tears rolled down her cheeks and she shook from the inside out. She thought she'd cried all she could over the weekend, but here she was Monday morning, still a blubbering mess. She'd cried more in the past three days than she had in her entire life.

"It's not your fault," Alex said, rubbing her back soothingly.

"It is," she insisted. "I should have put my foot down years ago. I should have made them take me seriously. Instead I came up with little deceptions to keep them placated. I did this to myself."

Alex plucked a tissue from her desk and pushed it into her hand. "And what does your millionaire have to say about all of this?"

Matt couldn't see the forest for the trees. He had become so obsessed with building this restaurant, nothing, not even her friendship would get in his way. And as much as that hurt her, she understood it in a weird way. She pitied him even. Matt was adrift—a lost soul looking for his place. Much as she was. No restaurant or business deal was going to fill the emptiness in his life.

Emily had spent most of the weekend at Alex's apartment, drowning in her misery. When she finally came home Sunday night, Matt had left a dozen messages on her answering machine. She'd erased them all without listening to a single one. She already knew what he would say, and she didn't want to hear again how much the restaurant meant to him.

"Matt will always be Matt," she told Alex now. "It will always be about making more money. About achieving more success. He'll never change."

"You're in love with him." It wasn't a question. It was a fact—one she couldn't deny.

"Maybe I am. Maybe we could have some sort of relationship, and for a while we might be happy. But eventually he would have to make a choice, and I already know what that choice would be. I'll never compromise myself for anyone again. From now on, it's about what I want."

"Your parents are damned lucky to have a daughter like you. If they can't see that, they're the ones with the problem."

Emily stepped up on her toes and pressed a kiss to Alex's cheek. "If you were straight, I'd ask you to marry me."

"And I'd say no. Because you're in love with someone else."

"Maybe it's a good thing Matt is buying the property," she said. "Without it he won't get his restaurant built, and we'd lose the account. Without the Touchdown account, the nursery would be history."

"You let me worry about the nursery for a while, okay?"

"After all that's happened, he may not want to work with me. He never signed a contract." She felt a rise of panic. She would never forgive herself if she were responsible for the demise of Marlette Landscape. She needed to secure the account. "What if he decided to take a bid from a different nursery?"

"That's not going to happen, Em."

"You don't know that."

"I think I do. From what I understand, Marlette was the only nursery bidding on the job."

Twelve

Matt stared blindly at his computer screen, unable to concentrate on a damned thing. He hadn't slept for days. His meticulously managed life was falling apart, yet the only thing he could think about, the only thing he *cared* about was that he'd hurt Emily deeply. He'd gone to her apartment four times Sunday, called and left messages begging to see her. And she'd ignored them all, making her feelings on the matter abundantly clear.

He'd lost. He hadn't even realized until then that this had been like a game to him. A challenge. Could he win Emily over? Could he make her bend to his will? Only when her parents offered him the property they were supposed to be saving for Emily did he realize the stakes. At first he'd actually thought he could reason with her, make her see that building his restaurant was the important thing. She could build her shop anywhere, couldn't she? But it wasn't about where or when or how much money it would cost. It was about faith and respect and loyalty.

None of which he'd shown her with any consistency.

In his life he'd never seen anyone look so defeated as Emily had when her parents had dismissed her dreams as silly then blamed her for Marlette Landscape's financial difficulties. He knew for a fact she was one hell of businesswoman—the glue that held the nursery together—yet he'd been so self-absorbed, so damned worried about building his restaurant that he hadn't come to her defense. And he hated himself for it.

He'd failed her. His betrayal was no less stinging than her parents'. He didn't deserve her friendship. But he'd give damn near anything to get it back. To get another chance.

There was a loud rap at his hotel-room door, then he heard Emily's voice.

"Matt, open up. I need to talk to you."

He jumped up so fast the chair he was sitting on tumbled over backward and crashed to the floor. He sprinted across the room, threw the deadbolt and swung the door open.

Emily stood in the hallway, dressed in her work clothes. She looked him up and down, frowned and said, "You look like hell."

He could have kissed her.

He dragged a hand across his beard stubble, through his tousled hair. Then he noticed the puffiness around her eyes and the joy at seeing her quickly dissolved. She'd been crying. Emily, who never cried, had been hurt that profoundly. By him.

Could this get any worse?

He held the door open for her. "Come on in."

"I can't stay long," she said, stepping inside and hovering near the door. "I just have to ask you a question."

"Okay."

"Is it true that there were no other nurseries bidding on the job?"

Just when he thought things couldn't get any worse. In her present state of mind, he knew she would misinterpret his motives. "Yes, it's true, but—"

Her eyes impaled him like two ice-blue daggers. "I would like nothing more than to tell you to take the account and shove it, Conway. I don't need your pity. But I have a responsibility to my employees."

"My hiring you has nothing to do with pity and everything to do with your competency. Yes, I knew you were having financial difficulties and the business would help, but I have a responsibility to my investors. If I didn't think you could handle the job, friend or not, I wouldn't even have considered you."

She narrowed her eyes at him. "That better be the truth."

He righted the chair on the floor and collapsed into it. "It's the truth, and it's a moot point now, seeing as how the restaurant may not be getting built."

"What are you talking about?"

"What do you mean, what am I talking about? Didn't you get my messages?"

She folded her arms across her chest. "I erased them all."

He laughed wearily and shook his head. Typical Emily. "The only solution I can find is to tear most of the building down and make it smaller, but my investors aren't real happy about it. It's pretty much a lost cause."

"But you'll have the extra property. You won't need to tear it down."

"See, if you'd listened to my messages you would already know, I'm not buying the property."

Emily couldn't believe what she was hearing. "What do you mean you're not buying it?"

"It belongs to you."

"But you heard my parents. They don't want to sell it to me. Just buy it, Matt. Save your restaurant."

"I can't do that. I don't want to do it. I already told them I'm not buying it. And I told them it was time they got their priorities straight. If they had any brains at all they would sell the property to you, as they promised. You're one hell of a good business-woman and it's time they saw that."

"You actually *said* that?"

"Yep."

"What did they say?"

A grin lifted the corner of his mouth and his dimple dented his cheek. "They were too stunned to say much of anything. Your mom did a fair amount of sputtering though."

She was feeling like sputtering herself. "But you *have* to buy it. Marlette can't lose this account. We're barely hanging on as it is."

Matt looked at her as if she had more than a few screws loose. "What does it matter? You're going to be leaving. You'll have your shop to run."

"Don't you see, without a job I'll never have the money to buy the property. I need six more months."

"I'm sure you can work something out with your parents. Some kind of payment plan."

She felt torn in half. On the one hand, she wanted to build her flower shop, but to deny Matt the property, she would be pounding the final nail in Marlette's coffin. "Why, Matt? Why would you do this for me? Do you feel as if you owe me?"

He shook his head, rubbing his eyes with the heels of his palms. "How does it always come back to that?"

"If that's the case, forget about it. You didn't love me. I got over it."

He leaned forward, his eyes dark and turbulent, and her breath caught in her throat. "Emily, do you want to know why I stopped calling, why I never came home?"

She nodded.

"My whole life, all I wanted was to get away from here. I wanted a fresh start in a place where no one knew me. Where I wasn't the son of two worthless drunks. I would have amounted to nothing here. Then that night on the beach happened and suddenly I had these feelings for you."

"Y-you had feelings for me?"

He stood, shoving his chair back. "Yeah, I had feelings for you, and they scared the hell out of me. I started thinking crazy things, like maybe I didn't want to leave. But I knew if I didn't, I'd be throwing my future away. I knew I wasn't good enough for you."

"Why would you think that?"

"I had nothing. I *was* nothing. You deserved better than that. Better than *me*."

She opened her mouth to speak, but no sound came out. Tears welled in her eyes and her throat squeezed shut. That's when she knew, when it became so completely clear to her. She was in love with Matt. The revelation filled her with equal parts joy and sadness because they had no future.

Even if she could never tell him, never say the words, she could at least show him.

Emily threw her arms around Matt's neck, nearly knocking him off his feet. She pulled his head down, locked her mouth on his and kissed the daylights out of him. He didn't think he'd ever been kissed with more enthusiasm than he had by Emily. She put her heart and soul and, in this case, her whole body into it.

He wrapped his arms around her and hugged her close to him. She felt too good, too perfect there. So good, he could imagine never letting go—even if that meant making sacrifices he'd never thought he would be willing to make.

When she finally broke the kiss, her lips and chin were pink and abraded from three days' growth of beard stubble.

"Is that the bedroom over there?" Emily asked, gesturing toward the bedroom door. When he nodded, she grabbed the front of his shirt and pulled him toward it. "Let's go."

"Emily, I'm a mess. I need a shower, and I need to shave."

"The shower." She made a purring noise deep in her throat. "Even better."

How they'd gone from her wanting to kill him, to her wanting to jump him was a mystery. Not that he was complaining. He wanted to spend the rest of the afternoon losing himself in that wonderful body of hers. Then tonight, after he took her out for a nice dinner, he wanted to do it all over again. He had eleven years of wanting her to make up for. Eleven years of dreaming about touching her. Eleven years of looking at the women in his arms and wishing they were someone else.

Wishing they were Emily.

Emily backed them into the bathroom and switched on the light. She smiled when she saw her choices: an enormous Jacuzzi tub or a two-headed shower stall wide enough to fit four people. "This just keeps getting better."

"Your choice." He peeled his T-shirt over his head.

"Both." She unfastened his pants, shoved them and his boxers down his legs. "Shower first, bath second."

He pulled her shirt up over her head and, after some minor fumbling, unhooked the clasp on her bra. Her breasts were perfectly rounded and deeply tanned, her nipples small and dusty rose. And there it was, that enticing nipple ring. Memories of it, of taking it into his mouth, had tortured him for days. They had invaded his dreams, filling them with erotic images. For two nights running he'd awoken aroused and restless and missing her more than he should have. Plagued by a hunger, a thirst, that only Emily could quench.

He brushed a finger across her nipple ring and Emily sighed and closed her eyes. He unsnapped her shorts and as he slid them down her legs he dropped to his knees. All that was left now was a strappy little thong, but he didn't remove it. Instead he pressed his cheek into the softness of her belly, against her sweetly scented skin. He loved the way she smelled, the way she tasted. The way she looked at him, with so much honesty and admiration, as if he were the center of her universe. That scared the hell out of him. What if he let her down again? Suppose he wasn't good enough?

She wrapped her arms around his head and for a minute they simply held each other. He needed her so deeply, so completely, he felt torn up inside. As if his guts had been ripped out, kicked around, then thrown back in upside down. He wasn't used to feeling this for anyone. Not in a very long time. Not since that first night on the beach. It was awful and wonderful at the same time.

He turned his head and she gasped, and he realized how rough his face must have felt against her tender skin. He pulled away. "I should shave first. I don't want to hurt you."

She cupped his cheeks in her hands. "I like you this way," she said. "It's sexy and dangerous."

"You like things dangerous, huh?" He slid his hands up the tops of her thighs and dipped his thumbs underneath each edge of the thong. Emily watched, eyes glazed with desire, as he hooked his fingers under the elastic band and eased the underwear down her legs. The skin under that barely there strip of fabric was golden, the hair pale and downy and soft to the touch.

Perfect.

"Condoms," she said suddenly. "Tell me you have some."

"In the bedroom." He pulled himself to his feet, wincing a little at the pinch of pain in his knee. "You get the shower ready and I'll go get them."

Emily watched his tight backside as he walked out

of the room, then she opened the shower door and turned on the water. She adjusted the temperature, testing it with the inside of her wrist, then stepped under the steamy spray.

Matt stepped in behind her, carrying several condom packets. He set them on the soap dish. "Mission accomplished. The rest of the box is by the sink just in case."

Emily watched as hot water sluiced down his body, over tanned ripples of muscle. He threw his head back into the spray to wet his hair, looking as if he belonged on the pages of a *Playgirl* magazine. She had to wonder again what a man like him was doing with a woman like her. A woman whose breasts were a touch too small and whose hips were a tad too wide. Yet he looked at her with nothing but appreciation and astonishment.

And hunger.

With a single look he could devour her—like the look he was giving her right now.

She grabbed a bottle of shampoo and poured some into her palm. "Turn around. I'll wash your hair."

He turned and let his head fall back. She rubbed the shampoo into that thick, dark hair and built up a lather, massaging his scalp and scratching lightly with her nails.

"That feels good," he said, his voice low and thick. "No one has ever done this before."

She rubbed the base of his skull and around his ears. "You've never had your hair shampooed when you get a haircut?"

"I go to a barber. The same one for, oh, ten years I think."

"You're a loyal customer."

Matt shrugged. "He does a good job."

She patted his shoulder. "Rinse."

He dipped his head under the water, rinsing the suds from his hair. While he did that, she grabbed a bar of soap, building a thick lather in her hands.

He shook the excess water from his hair and drew a hand across his face. "Do I get to do yours now?"

"Soon. Turn and face the wall."

He lifted an inquisitive brow, but did as she asked, bracing his hands against the tile wall. "You're not going to do anything kinky, are you?"

She propped her chin on his shoulder, smoothing her soapy hands up his chest, and said in a teasing voice, "I'll try anything at least once. What did you have in mind?"

"If I had any blood left in my brain I could answer that question. But if you'll let me turn around, I can show you."

A shiver of anticipation danced up her spine. "Not yet."

She drew his nipples between her slippery fingers, pinching lightly. He sucked in a sharp breath. She lathered the silky hair under his arms and the wide breadth of his shoulders, astonished by the solid muscle there. Women all over the world lusted after this man and right now he was all hers. And in a few weeks they would go their separate ways again. She hoped that this time they could part as friends.

Just maybe, if he could stay in Michigan… If he could put her before his career…

She shook away the thought. If she wasn't careful she would ruin what time they did have together. She was going to be thankful for their limited time. She was going to savor each and every minute and store it in her memory.

And darn it, she thought as a wave of emotion choked her, she was *not* going to cry.

"When do I get to wash you?" Matt asked.

"Soon," she promised, hoping her voice didn't betray her emotions. She lathered his back and rubbed herself against him, grazing his soapy skin with the hardened points of her breasts. She ran both hands down his tight, perfectly formed backside, then lower, and felt him shudder.

"Em—"

"Shh." She slipped her hands around to his firm, flat stomach, then down into the coarse hair at his groin. She reached lower still, carefully cupping him and he groaned.

He let his head drop, his forehead resting against the wall. "You wouldn't believe how amazing that feels."

She explored gently, purposely avoiding the one place she knew he wanted to be touched the most until finally he'd had enough. At least she assumed so when he spun around and pinned her to the adjacent wall. She gasped as her back hit the cold tile and Matt's mouth came down hard on her own. His beard was rough against her face, his mouth hot. She wrapped her arms around his neck, arched up, riding intimately against the hard length of him.

"We need a condom," he groaned against her lips. Breaking the kiss, he grabbed one from the soap dish, tore the package open with his teeth and she watched as he rolled it on. He really was magnificent. Everything about him was so strong and male. And so *large*. He was big all over.

"I love this," he said, reaching up to toy with her nipple ring. Then he lowered his head and took it between his teeth, tugging. Suddenly her legs didn't want to hold her up anymore, but that was okay, because Matt lifted her right up off her feet. She wrapped her legs around his waist and framed his face in her hands, locking her eyes on his as he slowly entered her. Inch by wonderful inch he filled her, the transition smooth and effortless because she was so completely ready for him. And when he'd buried himself as deeply as he could go, he stopped and for a long moment they simply held each other. She knew from the look in his eyes he was thinking the exact same thing she was—they were a perfect fit. And not just physically. Mentally, intellectually, spiritually—they were undeniably compatible. Except for the teensy problem of him being obsessed with his work and living a couple of thousand miles away.

Again she began to feel that deep sadness, that emptiness when she imagined her life without him in it. Then Matt began to move, so tenderly, his eyes still locked on hers. It was so beautiful, so magical, tears filled her eyes. She wanted to stay like this all night, Matt's hard body pressed against her, the hot water sharp on her sensitized skin. Her body was already trembling, screaming for release.

"Oh, Em." He pressed his forehead to hers and she could feel him tensing, feel him fighting to hold back for her and that simple act of selflessness was her undoing. She shuddered in his arms, crying out as sweet ecstasy swept over her. When she thought for sure Matt was only seconds behind her, he didn't stop. He drove deep and steady inside her until she felt the pressure begin to build once more. She hovered on the edge, not quite ready to tumble over, then Matt lowered his head, took her nipple ring in his mouth...

They shattered together, their release fierce and intense. They remained wrapped in each other's arms for several minutes afterward, until Matt's knee began to burn from the extra weight, but damn, he didn't want to let go yet. Each time he made love to Emily it was more special, more out-of-this-world fantastic.

His legs began to shake and Emily lifted her head from his shoulder.

"Your knee hurts," she said, sliding from his arms. "Why don't we go lie down?"

"Uh-uh," he said grabbing a bar of soap. "First I get to wash you. Turn and face the wall."

She assumed the position, then looked back at him over her shoulder. "Are you going to do something kinky?"

"Hell, yeah." He slid his soapy hands all over her back and across her shoulders.

She let out a long contented breath and her head dropped forward. "That's nice."

"I'm just getting started." He slid lower, down the sweet curve of her behind, and when she was soapy enough, he pulled her against him. She let out a little gasp of surprise when she realized he was very ready for her again. He was just as surprised. He had no idea he possessed that level of stamina anymore.

She pressed her backside erotically against the length of him. The slippery heat, the bold gesture, nearly did him in. He covered her breasts with his soapy hands. Their soft fullness fitting perfectly in his palms. He massaged gently, squeezing her nipples as she'd done to him. She moaned and pressed herself even harder against him.

He washed lower, down her hips and stomach, then he slipped a hand between her thighs and she shuddered in his arms. He filled her with one finger and she writhed against him—one more and she moaned. She was slick and hot and so ready for him he knew he had to have her again. And as much as he wanted to make love to her right there in the shower, he knew his knee would never last under the strain.

"I was thinking it might be time to move this into the bedroom," he said.

"Yes," she agreed breathlessly. "Let's go."

Thirteen

They stepped out of the shower, grabbed the box of protection from the bathroom counter, and fell into bed soaking wet.

For a while they only kissed, which was okay with Matt because no one kissed like Emily. Then their hands began to wander, and soon their mouths joined in on the action. They touched and tasted each other in a manner that would make most women blush. But not Emily. She couldn't seem to get enough—enough of touching him or of being touched. And when just touching wasn't enough, she straddled him and drove him deep inside her body.

He lost track of exactly how many times they made love, but when they finally took a break, when he was too exhausted to do any more than lie there like a lump, she sat up, bright-eyed, her hair adorably messy and said, "I'm starved. Want to go out and get a bite to eat?"

He looked up at her from his sprawled-out position on the rumpled sheets and thought, thank God for room service. Nothing short of a fire was going to get him out of this bed. "There's a menu by the phone. Knock yourself out."

She ordered sandwiches and beer, then sprawled out next to him while they waited for it to arrive. They didn't talk, just lay there quietly being together. He wondered what life would be like without this, and had a disturbing thought.

If the restaurant was no longer being built, he had no reason to stay in Michigan. It would be time to go back home soon.

He thought about returning to his life in L.A., and felt sick inside. What he had there wasn't a life. He'd never felt more alive, more complete, than these last few days with Emily. Where he belonged was in Chapel with her. *This* was home.

What he hadn't recognized before was so obvious to him now. No restaurant he could build, no business deal he could close would ever fill the void. What was missing from his life, what had been missing all these years, was her.

And he loved her. Deep down, he'd always known that, and he'd run from it.

It ended here. Today he stopped running.

"Emily, I—" He was interrupted by a loud knock, and cursed whoever had the lousy timing to interrupt them at that precise moment. "It's probably our room service. I'll just be a minute."

He rolled out of bed and tugged a pair of jeans

on. There was another loud knock and he yelled, "Hold on."

He shut the bedroom door partway behind him and yanked the suite door open, but instead of room service, Ty strutted past him and into the suite.

"I've got it," Ty said, waving a manila envelope.

"Got what?"

"The report from the P.I. All the dirt I need on Emily's boyfriend."

Matt swore silently. "Maybe now's not the time—"

"He's cheating on her." Ty pulled a stack of photos from the envelope and shoved them into Matt's hands. Then added with obvious disgust, "With a *guy*."

Matt glanced down at the pictures in his hands and—*Whoa!*—promptly handed them back. "You can have those back now."

"You're off the hook. You can stop trying to seduce Emily now."

Matt cringed, praying Emily wasn't hearing every word they were saying. "Ty, it wasn't—"

"My parents and I can't thank you enough for helping us. When we show Emily these pictures, she won't have a choice but to leave the guy. I'm taking them to my parents right now."

"You're not taking those pictures anywhere."

They both turned to see Emily standing in the bedroom doorway, fully dressed. She had that look on her face, that barely contained fury that told him he was in worse trouble than he'd thought. Matt cursed under his breath.

Ty paled about four shades. "You might have mentioned my sister was here, Matt."

"If you had shut up for two seconds I would have."

"I have an idea. Why don't you both shut up." Emily walked over to her brother and held out her hand. He actually cringed, as if he thought she might deck him. "Give me the envelope."

"I'm so sorry, Em," Ty said, handing her the photos. "You'll get over him. He wasn't good enough for you. You've got Matt now."

"No, I don't," she said, glancing at Matt, icy venom in her eyes. She dumped the contents of the envelope out on the table. She stuffed the negatives in her pocket and began tearing the photos.

"Hey!" Ty shouted.

"I can't believe you paid a private investigator to follow Alex. You've done some really stupid things in your life, but this definitely tops them all." Emily dumped the shredded photos in a trash can. "Are these all the pictures?"

"That's all of them. But tearing them up isn't going to change the fact that he's cheating on you, Em. You have to break up with him."

"Ty, you are such an idiot. Alex isn't my boyfriend, nor has he ever been."

"But you said—"

"I never said anything. You guys just assumed, and I never denied it."

"But—"

"Go home, Ty. Matt and I need to talk. Then I'm going to go explain everything to Mom and Dad. You *will not* say a word about this until I've talked to them, understand?"

Ty nodded and shrank toward the door, obviously intimidated by her threatening tone. "Okay. But when you're done talking to Mom and Dad, you're going to explain a few things to me.''

"Go," Emily said sternly, and her brother grudgingly left, flashing Matt a look of sympathy on his way out.

Matt shut the door and turned to Emily. Oh, man, he'd seen her mad before, but never like this. Her eyes had deepened to the steel-blue of his vintage '65 Mustang and he could swear he saw smoke coming out of her ears. "Give me a chance to explain."

"You know what my family is like, the way they try to control my life. And you were *helping* them? Pretending to be my friend so what, you could keep tabs on me for them?" She shook with anger. "You don't have to *seduce* me anymore? What is he, your pimp?"

"It wasn't like that, Emily." The words sounded lame, even to him. "I would have pursued you whether he put me up to it or not. I wouldn't have been able to stay away from you."

"I'm supposed to believe that?"

"I made a mistake. But your parents and Ty were really worried about you. They asked for my help. What was I supposed to tell them?"

"You could have told them no."

"How could I do that? If it wasn't for them, I wouldn't be where I am today. I owe them so much."

"Did it ever occur to you to *tell* me? Who were you protecting?"

"Your brother and your parents. And myself," he admitted, because to do otherwise would be a lie. "I was afraid you would be angry with me."

"Well, you were right, I'm angry."

"By helping them, I thought I was helping you."

"No, Matt, the only person you were trying to help was *you*. That's the way it's always been. I'm just sorry I didn't see it until now."

She turned to leave. He was losing her.

"Emily, wait! I know what it is. The thing that's missing from my life. I finally figured it out."

She stopped, her hand on the knob.

"It's *you*. You're the thing that makes me feel complete. I'm in love with you, Emily."

She stood very still for a long moment, then she turned to him, tears rolling down her cheeks. "The really sad thing is that I love you, too, Matt."

Then she was gone.

Matt stood in the empty lot next to Touchdown, watching the demolition team assemble.

"She'll cool down," someone said and he turned to see Ty standing behind him. "So this is it? You're just going to give up?"

Matt shrugged. "Not much choice. My investors all backed out and I can't take the risk of putting the money up myself. The weird thing is, all I can feel is relieved it's over. Building a restaurant here would have been a mistake. I knew it all along. I just wouldn't let myself see it."

"Matt, I wasn't talking about the restaurant."

Matt shoved his hands in his pockets. "I know what you were talking about."

"She'll come around."

"I don't think so. And honestly, I can't blame her if she hates me forever. I've done nothing but let her down since I've been back. I've screwed everything up."

"And every time you screw up, she forgives you. This is my fault, really. I shouldn't have stuck my nose in. I should have let nature take its course with you and Em."

"Nature? Do you mean you knew…"

"That something was going on with you two? Who didn't? You guys were attached at the hip since you were eight years old. Do you know how jealous I used to get? It was like you two had some secret club I wasn't invited into."

"We were just good friends," Matt said. Until the beach, anyway.

"When you left for college she was a wreck. I knew something happened between you. You made yourself pretty scarce for a long time and she spent way too much energy trying to pretend she didn't care. I must have asked her to come to California with me a dozen times, and she always said no. Getting you two back together was damn near impossible."

Matt could hardly believe what he was hearing. "Are you telling me you set this whole thing up?"

"More or less."

"What about the boyfriend? Was that just part of the plan?"

"No, that part was real. I didn't know they weren't really together. I just knew something about it wasn't right. She wasn't happy."

"And the part about him being into something illegal?" Matt asked.

Ty grinned. "Nah, I just made that up. You weren't looking like you were going to cooperate. I had to give you a good reason to want to help me."

Matt shook his head. "I fell for it."

"Yeah, you're pretty stupid that way. For all your success and your money, you had absolutely no direction. Those people you hang out with, the women you date—it's just not you. And Emily, man, she's just been a real pain in the rear since you left."

"Don't tell her that."

"Already did."

Matt raised an inquisitive brow. "What did you say exactly?"

"Everything that I'm telling you."

"And you walked away in one piece? How did you manage that? There's nothing she hates more than to have you and your parents messing with her life."

"I told her I did it because I was tired of seeing you both so unhappy. And I loved you both too much not to do something about it."

It wasn't often he and Ty displayed any kind of affection, and Matt found himself more than a little choked up. "What did Emily say?"

"She punched me in the stomach. Then she started crying and hugged me."

In the parking lot of Touchdown Matt heard a commotion and saw that the wrecking ball was in position. "This is it," he said.

"You're really going to let them do it? You're going to let them win?"

"It's not about winning or losing. The truth is, I don't care what anyone in this town thinks of me. I'm tired of trying to prove myself. I know what I've accomplished, and that's all that matters."

"What are you going to do next? Build another one somewhere else?"

He shook his head. "I don't think so. I'm thinking

of selling off the Touchdown chain. I've had a couple of decent offers. I may take some time off. Decide what I want to do next. But the thought of doing it alone…'' He shook his head, unable to speak for all the emotion backing up in his throat. He didn't want to do it without Emily by his side.

Ty clasped a hand on Matt's shoulder. ''Give her time. She'll come around.''

The foreman called out a warning to be sure the area was secure, and Matt took one last look at the building as the wrecking ball fell.

''How bad is it?'' Alex asked from his seat on the corner of Emily's desk.

''Bad,'' Emily said. ''If we stretch it, we can make it through to the end of the summer.''

Alex took a slug of his diet soda. ''Bummer.''

''Bummer?'' she repeated, barely able to contain her frustration. If her hand wasn't still sore from punching her brother, she would have broken Alex's nose. ''I tell you we're going to have to close our doors, putting our entire staff out of work, and all you can say is *bummer?* I've been killing myself trying to keep us in business.''

''And despite the odds you've done a valiant job. Give it up, honey.''

''I can't believe you're being so flip about this.''

''And I can't believe you still care. Your parents are selling you the property, you'll have your flower shop soon.''

''Yeah,'' she said grudgingly.

''You don't sound too happy about it anymore.''

She should have been ecstatic. Her parents were putting the property in her name next week on delivery of the first three-quarters of the money; the remaining amount to be paid in installments over the next two years. They were *finally* taking her seriously. The bank was considering her application, but had already said that with her impeccable credit and sound business plan they didn't think she would have any problems securing a business loan. She had everything she'd been working for, yet it held no satisfaction.

At first she'd blamed it on Conway. But after her talk with Ty this morning, she was having a really hard time holding on to her anger where he was concerned. Put in the identical position as Matt, she couldn't say she wouldn't have reacted as he had. The guy was loyal to a fault, though slightly misguided. And while she would have appreciated it if he'd told her the truth, she understood why he hadn't. She wanted to hate him for what he'd done. But all these sappy feelings of love kept mucking things up.

So if Matt wasn't the cause of her trepidation, what was the problem? That's when she'd realized, she wasn't unhappy about having a flower shop. She was unhappy about leaving Marlette. As stressful and crazy and frustrating as it could be at times, she loved her job. She worked nutty hours, not just for the money, but because she took so much pride in keeping the nursery on its feet. She was happy there, and even if she wouldn't be the one at the helm, she didn't want to leave until she knew they would open their doors for another season.

And Alex didn't seem to give a damn.

"Think big," Alex said, leaning closer. "If you could have anything in the world, *any* job, what would it be?"

She said without pause, "I would want a nursery like Marlette."

"Suppose you had a chance to buy Marlette? Would you?"

She could only dream it. It was completely out of her financial realm of comprehension. "I could never afford it. And even if I could, I'd be out of business before I started. We just don't have the clientele we used to."

"Suppose you had enough contracts lined up to keep you in business?"

"Alex, we both know that we've lost practically every bid this year. There are no guarantees."

"What if there were?"

He was leading her somewhere, and she wanted to know what he had up his sleeve. "Okay, what's the deal? What are you getting at? Do you know something about the lost bids?"

Alex grinned down at her. "Think about it, Em. How do you suppose I knew your millionaire didn't go to any other nursery. Who had access to all that information in those bids we lost?"

"It was you?" she asked, feeling as if she'd been poleaxed. "You were the one leaking the information?"

"I can't believe you didn't figure it out before this."

The betrayal she felt was so stark, so deep, she was numb with it. "Why would you do it? I worked so hard—"

"A business is always a better buy when it's about to go under. My mother is fed up and she wants to sell. You'll get it for a steal."

"Me?"

"Yes, *you*. You're going to buy Marlette."

"Are you telling me that you deliberately almost bankrupted the business just so *I* could afford to buy it?"

"I told you, I'm not as incompetent as you think."

"Are you nuts?" Emily could barely comprehend what he was telling her. And she couldn't believe he would do that for her. Marlette was his livelihood. His legacy. "What will you do? Where will you work?"

"Anywhere else. I've hated this God-awful business since the day my mother bought it. The only thing that kept me here this long is you and your passion for keeping it going. But I've had enough. I'm ready to move on."

She didn't know what to say. She couldn't even believe it was real. "But, is that fair to your mother?"

"My father left her a fortune when he died. She's not going to be hurting for money."

"But, what about clients?"

"I've got a dozen new clients contracted for the spring," he said. "So, what do ya' say?"

"Yes," she said, but it came out more like a squeal. She covered her mouth to contain a bubble of laughter. "Yes, I'll buy it."

"I'll let my mother know and get the ball rolling."

She was going to own Marlette Landscape. It could be Douglas Landscape or anything else she wanted to call it. It would be all hers. She could barely suppress her excitement. Her office walls were the only thing keeping her from going in a dozen directions at once. She could hardly wait to tell Matt—

And just like that, her bubble burst. She wouldn't be seeing Matt again. Not even as friends. It would be too hard, hurt too much. She'd already decided it would be best for them both if they cut all ties. Even if she could forgive Matt, which she was sure she could, they would never have any kind of life together. She had a business tying her to Chapel and he had a life—superficial as it was—in California. Business would forever dominate his time, and she would always feel as if she were in second place. She was finished compromising herself. For once in her life, she wanted to be number one.

There was no point in dwelling on it any longer. She had a nursery to run. From this day forward, Matt was out of her life.

"I'll have to call my parents, tell them I won't be needing the property—" She gasped and shoved herself up from her chair. "Oh, no!"

"What?" Alex shouted, nearly falling off the edge of her desk. "What's wrong?"

"I don't need the property. Oh my God, what time is it?"

Alex checked his watch. "Three-fifteen."

She fumbled in the file cabinet for her purse. "I have to hurry. I have to stop them."

"Stop who?"

"The demolition crew! They're going to tear it down today. Matt can buy the property!" She found her purse and rummaged through it. "Oh, where are my keys?"

Alex hopped off her desk and yanked his keys out of his pocket. "I have no idea what you're talking about, but it sounds exciting. I'll drive you there."

Fourteen

She was too late.

By the time she got there, Touchdown was gone. The only thing left was an enormous pile of rubble. And even that was fast disappearing as a crew dumped the remains in enormous trucks to be hauled away.

"That's one big heap of garbage," Alex said, shaking his head. "What a waste."

"You missed the show."

Emily turned to see Ty walking up behind them. "When did they do it?"

"Noon."

"How is Matt taking it?"

"Why don't you ask him yourself? He's at his hotel packing."

Emily squelched the sudden rush of panic rising

up in her at the thought of Matt leaving Chapel forever.

It's over, she reminded herself yet again. He couldn't stay and she couldn't go with him. It was hopeless.

Ty nodded to Alex. "How's it going?"

Alex returned the nod, adding a touch of flair. "It's been better, and you?"

"You know," Ty said with a shrug, then added, "So, you're gay?"

Alex's brow quirked up with surprise at the blatant question. "Why, you interested?"

Ty's eyes widened and he took a step away. Emily had to bite her lip not laugh.

Alex rolled his eyes. "A homophobe. Great. Don't worry, fly boy, my heart belongs to another."

"Behave," Emily said, and turned to her brother. "When is he leaving?"

"When is who leaving?"

"*Matt.*"

Ty frowned. "Matt's not leaving."

"But you said he was packing."

"He is packing, to move into his rental house."

Emily suddenly felt dizzy, as if the world had shifted on its axis. "Rental house?"

"I found him a place this afternoon. He's decided to stay in Michigan for a while."

It doesn't mean anything, she told herself. Not a single thing. He would leave eventually. He had a business to run. A life in California.

When she didn't acknowledge him, Ty added, "He's even talking about selling the Touchdown chain and taking some time off."

"Oh." She tried to swallow, but all the moisture in her mouth had evaporated.

"Is that all you can say? *'Oh.'*"

Right now, she couldn't say anything. Her heart was beating way too hard and fast for her to think straight.

"It's been five days," Ty said, draping an arm over her shoulder. "Don't you think you've tortured the guy enough? He wants a reason to stay. He loves you for cripes sake."

"But what if he decides to go back? What then?"

Ty shrugged. "You'll work it out."

"Though it pains me to say it, I'm afraid I have to agree with your brother," Alex said. "At least go talk to him."

Matt might not be going back to Los Angeles. He might be selling his restaurants. He'd told her he loved her, that she was what was missing in his life.

Could the message be any clearer?

"Alex," she said. "I need your keys."

Matt dropped his bags in the doorway and looked around the foyer of his rental house. Rental cars, rental houses—he really needed to get some permanence in his life. Tomorrow he would go out and buy a car. And if anyone gave him a reason to stay in Michigan permanently, he might look into having a house built. Something that *wasn't* a mansion.

But as rental houses went, this one wasn't too bad. When his furniture arrived, it would be downright livable.

"Kind of small, isn't it?"

Matt spun around and almost tripped over his luggage. His heart did an end-to-end flip when he saw

Emily in the doorway, a potted fern hanging from each hand.

"You think it's too small?" he asked, following her gaze up the vaulted ceiling in the great room, over the stone fireplace and slate mantel and beyond to the formal dining room.

She took a few steps in, looking around. "Are you kidding, I have closets bigger than this."

A twenty-two-hundred-square-foot closet? Even he didn't have one *that* big. He nodded to the ferns. "Friends of yours?"

"Oh." She looked down, as if she'd forgotten she was holding them. "These are for you. I heard you might be in town for a while and thought you might like the company. You know, someone to talk to."

She was fishing, big-time. Pumping him for information. Let her sweat a little, he decided. God knows she'd made him sweat his share this past week. "Thanks. They'll look great in the kitchen." He took them from her, his fingers brushing hers in the process. It was all he could do not to drag her into his arms and never let go.

He set the plants on the brick floor leading into the kitchen. "I heard from Ty that you talked with your parents. How did that go?"

"As well as can be expected, I guess. I've promised to be honest with them and they've promised not to nitpick and stick their noses in where they don't belong. It may take some time, but I think they're coming around." She took a few more steps in, wedging her hands into her shorts pockets. "It's really beige in here, huh?"

"Yeah, rentals are funny that way. I figure I won't

be here long enough to paint, though, so I'd better get used to it. I only have a three-month lease.''

That wasn't what she wanted to hear, though she was trying damned hard not to let her disappointment show. She took a step back toward the door. ''So, you'll be going back to California?''

''Maybe, maybe not. It just depends on whether or not I have a good reason to stay.''

''Like…a job?''

''Maybe.''

She nodded, looking thoughtful. ''I hear they're hiring at the Dairy-O on Main Street.''

''Really. Sounds…challenging.''

''Of course, that's only seasonal. They shut down during winter.''

Grinning, Matt took a couple of steps toward her. ''I was thinking of something a little more permanent than that. Something with an emotional attachment.''

She took a few steps in his direction, her brow crinkled in thought, then she brightened. ''I know. You could get a dog. Or a cat.''

''I could do that.'' He closed the last few spaces between them, and gently pulled her to him. She just about melted into his arms. She smelled so good and felt so right, he didn't know how could have missed it before. ''Or, I could get a wife.''

Head against his chest, she nodded. ''You could get one of those.''

''And maybe a couple of kids?''

She looked up at him, eyes narrowed. ''I don't know about that.''

''Not necessarily right away,'' he added.

''So there's no confusion here, you are talking

about us, right? Because I'm going to feel really stupid if some supermodel pops out of the kitchen."

He couldn't stop the goofy grin from spreading over his face. He'd be damned if this wasn't exactly where he wanted to be. "I'm definitely talking about us."

"What about L.A.?"

"California just isn't where I want to be anymore. I don't know if it ever was. Everything I could want—have *ever* wanted—is right here, in Chapel."

"I thought you hated it here."

"So did I. But it's who I am, and I realized, you can't run from who you are. I'm staying, and if there's anyone who doesn't like that, it's too damned bad."

She squeezed him harder and sighed. "You should know, I have a career to think about. You're looking at the future owner of Marlette Landscape."

There was no mistaking the satisfaction in her eyes, or his own feelings of pride. "Congratulations."

"I'll be really busy, so don't get any ideas about keeping me barefoot and pregnant."

"If we did—have kids I mean—maybe I could stay at home with them part of the time."

Her brow crinkled. "You? What about work?"

"In another couple of weeks Touchdown is going to belong to someone else. We're negotiating the contracts right now. I figured it was time I tried something different. Something a little less demanding on my time. I've got all this money, I might as well enjoy it. Right?"

"What would you like to do?"

"I've been thinking about that a lot. I got a degree

in physical education as a fallback, and I hear the coach over at the high school is talking about retiring. I've really missed the game, so I thought, what the heck, I could apply for the position.''

"A high-school football coach?''

He frowned. "You don't think so?''

"No, I think you'd be a great coach. You'll be good at whatever you choose to do because that's the kind of man you are.''

He hoped he was good enough for Emily. Good enough to keep her happy. This was all new to him. He didn't want to screw it up. "I can't promise that I won't say or do something dumb and hurt your feelings every now and then, even if I don't mean to. I'm going to make mistakes, Emily.''

"And I can't promise that I won't lock you out of the bedroom and make you sleep on the couch for a day or two. But I'll forgive you eventually.'' She looked up at him, his entire future shining in the blue of her eyes. "I'll always forgive you, because I love you, Matt.''

"I love you, too, Em.''

He couldn't hold back any longer. He cupped the back of her neck with one hand, nudged her chin up with the other, and proceeded to kiss her socks off.

This is it, he thought as he savored the sweetness of her mouth, the silky softness of her hair in his fingers. This was his for the rest of his life. He'd finally found it, that feeling of utter contentment he'd been searching for.

Hard to believe, it had been waiting for him all this time, right in Emily's arms.

* * * * *

introduces an exciting new family saga
with

DYNASTIES: THE DANFORTHS

A family of prominence...
tested by scandal, sustained by passion!

Available at your favorite retail outlet.

If you enjoyed what you just read,
then we've got an offer you can't resist!

Take 2 bestselling
love stories FREE!

Plus get a FREE surprise gift!

Clip this page and mail it to Silhouette Reader Service™

IN U.S.A.
3010 Walden Ave.
P.O. Box 1867
Buffalo, N.Y. 14240-1867

IN CANADA
P.O. Box 609
Fort Erie, Ontario
L2A 5X3

YES! Please send me 2 free Silhouette Desire® novels and my free surprise gift. After receiving them, if I don't wish to receive anymore, I can return the shipping statement marked cancel. If I don't cancel, I will receive 6 brand-new novels every month, before they're available in stores! In the U.S.A., bill me at the bargain price of $3.80 plus 25¢ shipping and handling per book and applicable sales tax, if any*. In Canada, bill me at the bargain price of $4.47 plus 25¢ shipping and handling per book and applicable taxes**. That's the complete price and a savings of at least 10% off the cover prices—what a great deal! I understand that accepting the 2 free books and gift places me under no obligation ever to buy any books. I can always return a shipment and cancel at any time. Even if I never buy another book from Silhouette, the 2 free books and gift are mine to keep forever.

225 SDN DZ9F
326 SDN DZ9G

Name	(PLEASE PRINT)	
Address	Apt.#	
City	State/Prov.	Zip/Postal Code

Not valid to current Silhouette Desire® subscribers.

Want to try two free books from another series?
Call 1-800-873-8635 or visit www.morefreebooks.com.

* Terms and prices subject to change without notice. Sales tax applicable in N.Y.
** Canadian residents will be charged applicable provincial taxes and GST.
All orders subject to approval. Offer limited to one per household.
® are registered trademarks owned and used by the trademark owner and or its licensee.

DES04R   ©2004 Harlequin Enterprises Limited

COMING NEXT MONTH

#1627 ENTANGLED—Eileen Wilks
Dynasties: The Ashtons
Years ago, Cole Ashton and Dixie McCord's passionate affair had ended when Cole's struggling business had taken priority over Dixie. Now, she was back in his life and Cole hoped for a second chance. But even if he could win Dixie once more, would Cole be able to make the right choice this time?

#1628 HER PASSIONATE PLAN B—Dixie Browning
Divas Who Dish
Spunky nurse Daisy Hunter never thought she'd find the man of her dreams while on the job! But when a patient's relative, athlete Kell McGee, arrived in town, she suddenly had to make a difficult decision—stick to her old agenda for finding a man or switch to passionate Plan B!

#1629 THE FIERCE AND TENDER SHEIKH—Alexandra Sellers
Sons of the Desert
Sheikh Sharif found long-lost Princess Shakira fifteen years after she'd escaped her family's assassination. As the beautiful princess helped heal her homeland, Sharif passionately worked on mending Shakira's spirit. Though years as a refugee had left her hardened, could the fierce and tender sheikh provide the heat needed to melt Shakira's cool facade and expose her heart?

#1630 BETWEEN MIDNIGHT AND MORNING—Cindy Gerard
When veterinarian Alison Samuels moved into middle-of-nowhere Montana, she hardly expected to start a fiery affair, especially with hunky young rancher John Tyler. To J.T., this tantalizing older woman was a stimulating challenge and Alison was more than game. But J.T. hid a dark past and Alison wasn't one for surprises....

#1631 IN FORBIDDEN TERRITORY—Shawna Delacorte
Playboy Tyler Farrel was totally taken when he laid eyes on the breathtakingly beautiful Angie Coleman. She was all grown up! Despite their mutual attraction, Ty wouldn't risk seducing his best friend's kid sister until Angie, sick of being overprotected, decided to step into forbidden territory.

#1632 BUSINESS AFFAIRS—Shirley Rogers
When Jenn Cardon placed the highest bid at a bachelor auction, she had no idea she'd just landed a romantic getaway with sexy blue-eyed CEO Alex Dunnigan—her boss! Thanks to cozy quarters, sexual tension turned into unbridled passion. Alex wasn't into commitment but Jenn had a secret that could keep him around...forever.

SDCNM1204